I0556187

THE FIRSTS

A GUZZI LEGACY
COMPANION NOVEL

BETHANY-KRIS

Copyright © 2020 by Bethany-Kris. All Rights Reserved.

WARNING: The unauthorized reproduction or distribution of this copyrighted material is illegal and punishable by law. No parts of this work may be reproduced, copied, used, or printed without expressed written consent from the publisher/author. Exceptions are made for brief excerpts used in reviews.

Published by Bethany-Kris

www.bethanykris.com

ISBN 13: 978-1-989658-33-8

Editor: Elizabeth Peters

Cover Design © Lee Ching, Under Cover Designs

This is a work of fiction. Names, characters, places, organizations, corporations, locales and so forth are a product of the author's imagination, or if real, used fictitiously. Any resemblance to a person, living or dead, is entirely coincidental.

For fans of the Guzzi boys ... XO.

CONTENTS

CORRADO, ALESSIO & GINEVRA: PART 1

1.

Ginevra

THE only *good* thing about Thursdays? Her classes at college ended early enough that when Ginevra returned home, she usually had a couple of hours *alone*. A feat, considering between her two sisters, Corrado, *and* Alessio, someone was always there. Or coming and going. Or even better, inviting people over which meant a revolving line of guests.

Usually, Ginevra didn't mind that. Except when she had a week like this one where she was simply ready for the weekend and didn't want to *people*.

It didn't help that she'd been without both her boys for a couple of weeks because they had business to handle in Vegas with The League. The more time she spent away from one or both of them, the worse her mood became.

Considering how kind Ginevra was any other time, that really said something because she was ready to bite off anyone's head who stepped in her way. Especially when all she wanted to do at the moment was go straight upstairs, sink into a hot bath, and call Corrado and Les.

"Why the scowl, kitten?"

Ginevra's head snapped up in the entry hallway of their double-wide brownstone at the voice she hadn't been expecting to hear. After all, both men were in Vegas and should still be there for at least another week or more.

And yet, there stood Les.

Alessio grinned her way from the end of the entry where he leaned against the doorway leading into the living room. He looked like her wettest dream standing there in a leather jacket—complete with all the buckles and spikes he loved—and black jeans that molded to those muscular thighs of his. The plain white T-shirt he'd thrown on was just tight enough to the bands of muscles that made up the hardness of his chest that she let out a quick exhale.

These men.

This one.

Corrado.

Both of them.

They drove her crazy.

Constantly.

"When did you get home?" she asked.

Alessio shrugged one shoulder. "Today. Wanted to surprise you. I got out of work a little early."

"Corrado didn't want you to stay in Vegas?"

"Why, so you can be lonely here?"

"Bet he's lonely there, now."

"He's a big boy," Alessio replied, that grin of his turning sinful in a blink. "And he'll be home soon."

"Yeah?"

Les nodded. "Yeah, babe."

Good.

They were good like this. But everything was better when they were all together.

"So, how much longer are you going to stand all the way down there looking at me when we both know you would much rather be down here with *me*?" Alessio asked, tipping his head to the side like he was encouraging her to move and *fast*. "Because it's been a month since I've had my hands on you, and I'm not okay with that."

Ginevra gulped down a breath. "Oh?"

"Not at all."

She didn't need him to tell her again. Those high-heeled boots of hers smacked against the wall when they came off. Her coat hit the floor right along with her purse instead of hanging from her designated hook like they should be—better things were waiting at the end of the hall, anyway.

Alessio's arms were already open and waiting to hide her away from the rest of the world the second she

2

reached his spot. Leather, smoke, and just a *hint* of the spicy, crisp cologne Corrado wore soaked into her lungs when she breathed him in. No doubt, before he left Vegas, Alessio had seen Corrado and that was how he lingered behind, too.

For a moment, she could pretend they were both home.

Les's mouth pressed to the top of her head with a soft kiss while his arms stayed tight like steel bars around her. He didn't push; he simply waited for her to take what she wanted. Something else the three of them seemed to find worked best for all of them.

Tipping her head back, Ginevra pushed up to her tiptoes and closed the distance remaining between them, so she could have that mouth of his on *hers*. His tongue tasted like the cherry soda he always grabbed from the store down the street from their brownstone, but with just a hint of whiskey.

A drink he hated. Corrado's *favorite*. Yet, it was the *only* drink he'd have when Corrado wasn't home. Ginevra didn't pretend to understand all the nuances of her boys and the side of their relationship that was just the two of them, but then again … she didn't have to. Besides, they were teaching her.

One thing at a time.

Alessio's kiss took her away from the world all over again. She swore even the brownstone drifted away while their kiss became a war. What had been a simple hello quickly turned into hot torture with every slide of his tongue along with hers like he was teasing and promising all at the same time.

"You're just … *wicked*," she breathed when he pulled away just enough to dot kisses along the line of her jaw. Of course, that path of his continued down the side of her throat to where the neckline of her dress dipped low to show off a bit of cleavage. "And you know it. Don't even say hello properly—just move right on to *this*."

"This is how I say hello, kitten."

3

That time, his *kitten* came out husky.

And hot.

Yep.

"What do I have to do to get you bent over the back of the couch, huh?" Alessio asked.

Ginevra could have played coy.

She didn't really want to.

"Say the words," she replied.

Alessio's gaze lifted to meet hers, and a dark gleam zoned in on her. That look in his eyes was enough to have her thighs clenching. "Five seconds to get there with your dress hiked up and your panties down to your ankles, then, or I'll do it for you myself."

Ginevra flashed her teeth with her smile, challenging him since she knew this would end *very* well for her. "I'll see what I can do."

That hand of his cracked against the curve of her ass when she passed him by to head into the living room. Alessio did exactly as he promised, too, by bending her over the couch in less than five seconds after she entered the living room. Of course, he took the chance to kiss her on the way over before shoving her roughly over the back of the plush leather.

Then, when he realized the skirt of her dress was a tight, non-stretchy fabric that he couldn't get shoved up around her waist, he simply ripped it right down the back at the zipper to where it stopped at the curve of her lower back. Only then did he let her step out of it.

Nothing else, though.

Not even the black cotton panties with the lace trim that matched the bralette he shoved his hands up under while demanding, "Pull those panties aside and get me inside you."

How in the midst of undressing her that he managed to partially undress himself, Ginevra didn't know. It spoke to the distraction Alessio could be—the *force* he truly was when he leveled one hundred percent of himself on someone else.

Every charming, broken, *sexy* piece that made him ... well, *him*.

The first night she met Alessio, she had called him overwhelming to Corrado. That hadn't been a lie, and honestly, not one goddamn thing had changed in that regard. Not that Ginevra wanted him to change. Like this, she thought he was *always* at his best.

Which was why she did exactly what he demanded of her, without question and all too happily, because of how she knew it would end. With her *pleased*, blissed, and over every stressful thing that had happened throughout the week.

That was what Les did for her. Corrado, too, when he was there. And *fuck*, when it was both of them? She didn't stand a damn chance.

The second she had her panties shoved aside and Alessio's cock filling her, Ginevra swore the rest of the world disappeared. All that mattered was the way he fucked her while grabbing onto her tits with one hand and shoving two fingers of his other into her mouth for her to suck and bite at that same time.

She was grateful he managed to get home when the house was empty because there was nothing quiet about them together. Not her sounds, or the brutal rhythm of his fucking. Her sisters still lived with her, although they spent an equal amount of time with her as they did Siena, and wouldn't be home for an hour or more yet.

"Oh, my God, *Alessio*," Ginevra mumbled into the palm of his hand as he pounded her through her first orgasm. "Holy shit ... *yes*."

He only slowed as her tremors did.

And it was just enough for her to hear the husky clearing of a throat that had her lifting her head. There, on the side table was the laptop facing them. On the screen was Corrado with a grin that told her he very much enjoyed the scene he just got from the two of them.

It wouldn't be the first time.

Wouldn't be the last, either.

"Planned that, did you?" she dared to ask.

Alessio's soft fingertips dragged down her stomach before grazing over her hips and settling on her ass. "Had to give him something."

"Lucky me," Corrado replied, entirely unashamed.

"Well," Ginevra drawled, her gaze drifting to the man grinning on the screen of the laptop and then back over her shoulder to the one that was now peppering her shoulder with hot kisses, "that *was* nice."

"You were right, Corrado. It was a good idea."

Corrado chuckled at Les's declaration. "Do you know how much easier *many* things would be if you just said those words a bit more often?"

"Where's the fun in that?"

"What idea?" Ginevra asked.

Alessio's hands flexed on her tender ass, and the motion had his still-hard cock twitching inside her. A shiver raced over her spine. "*This.*"

Ah.

She understood.

"Not as much fun for him, though, when he's in Vegas."

"Depends on how you look at it." Corrado winked on the screen. "You know, seeing as how this is a recorded call that goes to my cloud, and I can refer back to it—"

"You will delete it by *tomorrow morning*," she said.

God knew she didn't need *that* out into the world. Like her neighbors didn't already give the three of them a side eye when all they did was walk down the fucking street. Or her *first* gyno who asked far too many questions about her sex life. Maybe that one was all for the sake of the medical side of things, but still …

Ginevra understood the curiosity. That didn't mean she fed it, however, because their life together wasn't meant for the public's entertainment.

Corrado hummed under his breath. "Nothing gets deleted from the cloud."

"Well ... *it better.*"

The boys' laughter coated the room, and all over again, she wished Corrado was back home from The League because things were easier when they were all together. She wouldn't demand it of him not when they never demanded anything more from her than she was willing to give. She was pretty sure his job was something she shouldn't put restraints or demands on.

"Thursdays are always the worst for you," Corrado said, his tone still thick with his lust. "You've had enough of *everyone's* shit by then, though you won't say it, and you know you still have one more day left to get through before it's the weekend."

"He's not wrong," Les murmured.

"*Now,*" Corrado added thickly, "if you could just come around to the other side of the couch and let me see how wet and pink that pussy of yours is before he fucks you again, that'd be *perfect.*"

Ginevra smiled.

Les nipped her shoulder, saying, "We can do that."

No, they weren't the norm.

She still loved it.

2.

CORRADO loved how he had managed to get home to New York for what seemed like a blink before The League called him back with an assignment from a client that *demanded* he be on the team for it. He had a month back with Les and Ginevra, or just about, and then he was on a flight headed for Vegas.

Except he didn't fucking love it at all.

"I'm starting to think I need to retire," Corrado grumbled into the phone.

Alessio's chuckles didn't just reach through the speakers, but all through his lover, too. It made Corrado wish he was back across the country, so he could give Les something to *really* laugh about while he held the man down to a flat surface.

Even better if Ginevra joined.

Yeah.

Vegas was not where he wanted to be.

At all.

"Dare wouldn't let that happen, and to make him happy, Cree would be the one to deliver the news because he'd have fun doing that, too," Alessio replied.

Corrado sighed. "Probably, the bastards."

"Could work them into the idea, though."

"Keep talking. You always have the best plans."

That dark chuckle of Alessio's had Corrado's dick perking to life under his slacks as he headed into the walk-in closet of the master bedroom in their Vegas penthouse. They had yet to bring Ginevra to the place, but that was only because there seemed to be so little time for them to do anything.

That, and she didn't want to leave her sisters for that

long. They had school, and everything else … well, frankly all of them had to be a little creative when it came to being together.

"We'll get back to the idea," Les told him. "Give it time."

"*Right.*"

"What are you doing right now?"

"Trying to find the right tie."

He swore he could see Alessio shaking his head when he replied, "Would it kill you to wear a pair of jeans to work?"

"Yes, it would."

"Even just to … ditch the blazer one time?"

"It's a Guzzi thing."

"The only time you don't wear suits is in bed and when you work out," Alessio said. "I don't understand it at all."

"I intend to look like I have money because I do, Les."

"And comfort means—"

"What is comfortable about jeans and *leather*? Especially in the heat of fucking *Nevada.*"

"Uh … everything?"

"Right. You do hear yourself, yeah," Corrado drawled. "We'll get back to this argument that goes in circles every time we have it because I don't have time this morning. Dare has already called me three times after he woke me up. The bastard knew I came in on a red-eye, and yet he still wanted me there at eight this morning. I don't even roll out of bed before—"

"Nine, closer to ten if you can help it. Yeah, we *all* know. He must be fine with risking your mood at getting you there early, then."

"Listen, my moods are—"

"Pretty fucking hot when you're fucking yourself out of it with one of us. Not so great when you're alone and everyone knows it, man."

Corrado sighed.

Les had a point.

"So, again, Dare must be willing to risk it. How many hours of sleep did you get?"

"Arrived at the penthouse around five."

"*Ouch.*"

"Fuck it," Corrado muttered. "Is what it is."

"What's the job?"

"The return of ... something. A painting? Maybe it's a sculpture. Dare might have said, but Cree was in the background bitching like he does, and you know how I tune them out."

"We all do," Les said dryly.

"Anyway, it's a lot of money and he knows she's moving it in the coming weeks. Buddy's wife took it in the divorce when it wasn't hers to take. Renzo is going in with an explosive device he's been working on. Minimum damage, maximum impact."

"And you all have to move fast."

"Yeah, so—"

"Shit," Alessio grunted on the other end of the call. "I gotta run to Siena's and grab the girls for Ginevra. I wasn't watching the time."

"Does that mean Ginevra's still in bed?"

A quiet laugh answered his question.

"I wish," Les muttered.

"What does that mean?"

After Corrado had managed to make it home and was there for a couple of weeks, Ginevra ended up with a fucking ear infection. He blamed it on New York weather and the stress she had to deal with between handling her sisters, decorating a huge home, going to school, and *them.* Nonetheless, that infection then went down to her throat. It took Corrado three days of *bitching* before she finally agreed to go to the hospital.

Lucky for her because Alessio was an hour away from calling a doctor to come to them. Antibiotics and bed rest got her back on her feet, but they both thought she needed more time to relax before she got back to it all.

Clearly, Ginny disagreed.

What could they do?

The woman was grown.

"She felt good enough to go to classes today," Les said.

"Well, you're a far better nurse than I am, so ..."

"Right."

The scoff that accompanied Les's statement had Corrado grinning.

"Doesn't matter," Alessio added after a moment, "I know exactly how to keep that woman in bed when she needs to be there. Easier now that she's feeling better."

Yeah.

Corrado heard the suggestion.

Every single bit of it.

"Don't tempt me to tell Dare and Cree to fuck off so I can fly home," Corrado said. "You know good and well what you're doing saying shit like that to me."

Alessio laughed. "Of course, I do. Gives you something to get this job done faster for—where's the problem?"

"Mmm."

"They called me, too, by the way. Dare and Cree, I mean."

"A new recruit, yeah?"

"So I was told. That was my agreement. Handle the trainees with Cree ... stay on the continent."

"I could do that," Corrado said.

"What happened to retirement?" Les asked.

"Working my way to it."

"Sure, sure. I gotta go."

Corrado didn't want to hang up.

"Call me later," he said to Les, "and get Ginny on the phone."

"She *is* feeling better."

"*Still.*"

"Will do. Love you."

Corrado smirked. "Too much, Les."

"Absolutely."

3.

Alessio

"WHAT are you—"

"*Shut up.*"

That was all Alessio heard Corrado say before the man was in the shower with him. His back hit the wall with a *thump*. The ache in his spine made him answer Corrado back with the same roughness when his lover's mouth landed against his, and Alessio dragged his bottom lip between his teeth.

Just enough for Corrado to feel the sting.

"*Fuck*," he grunted into Alessio's kiss. "That's what I wanted."

Him, too.

After a month of the two of them running back and forth between New York and Vegas, never once getting more than a day here and there—a week, once, because they were lucky—to enjoy each other's company … this was exactly what the two of them needed. Not to mention, Les only had a few more days in New York with Corrado and Ginevra before he had to head back to Vegas.

After all, his trainee was still in *training*. He got these few days off from The League by the skin of his fucking teeth, and he didn't want to waste a second of it.

Alessio groaned when Corrado's hand found his cock wet from the shower and already hard to stroke tightly in his warm palm. "Jesus Christ."

"Quiet," Corrado warned, "because someone is sleeping and sick."

Right.

Like he needed the reminder.

Ginevra woke up feeling nauseous the morning before, and it only stopped long enough for her to sleep. They weren't quite sure what was wrong, and she didn't want to go to the doctor. Not a surprise because she *never* wanted to go to the doctor.

He'd get her there.

Later.

After her nap.

Yeah.

But right then, he was more interested in the way Corrado kissed and bit his way down the corded muscles of Alessio's throat to his chest before continuing even lower. Anticipation curled hot and heavy in his stomach making every single one of his muscles clench with what he knew was coming next.

His dick.

Corrado's mouth.

Fast, hard shower sex.

It'd been a while.

Probably too long.

"*Fucking hell,*" Alessio breathed when Corrado finally lowered enough to catch his cock with his mouth. His hand stayed there too, tight to the base while the heat of his lover's mouth took him deep enough to take his breath away. "Can't be quiet like—"

Corrado let him go.

Even his mouth.

Alessio felt that fucking *everywhere.*

"*Try.*"

"*God.* Fuck you, man."

Corrado's laughter coated the large shower before he was right back to sucking Alessio's dick like water was about to come out of the tip. His head fell back to the cool tiles on the wall, so he could avoid the spray of hot water *and* watch Corrado at the same time.

Alessio's hands found their way into Corrado's damp hair. He twisted and tugged while Corrado swallowed him deeper, and his teeth teased the sensitive underside of Alessio's shaft. He didn't pretend to have any kind of control when this man was sucking him off because he had none.

Not like this.

Goddamn.

There was always something about the way Corrado watched Alessio when he was on his knees for him that *really* did it for him. The pleased, *knowing* glint in Corrado's dark eyes that told him the man understood it was him beneath the other, but he still had all the fucking power in that moment.

The control to make Les lose it.

To make him blow.

All of it.

For the moment.

It might take nothing more than a blink for the power to shift and change when the two of them were like this, but not right now. He liked this perfectly fine.

Letting go of Corrado's hair, Les shoved his fingers into his own as the tightness in his balls increased, and he climbed closer. *Nearly fucking there.* He was pretty sure he even told Corrado that, but he couldn't hear anything.

Nothing but the shower.

And his own heartbeat.

It all thundered.

"*Shit, Corrado, don't you dare—*"

Corrado dragged his teeth from the base of Alessio's cock all the way to the tip before sucking him in deep again. That was all it took to make him empty his balls.

God love Corrado …

Because the man took it all.

He looked damn good doing it, too.

"Swear you just do this shit to me to—"

"Hear you say my name like that," Corrado said, his laughter thick with the need to fuck as he stood straight and kissed Les hard. There was something about the taste of himself on Corrado's tongue when it swept against his own that had his cock jerking all over again. "Absofucking-lutely. Also, looks like someone is feeling better."

Les looked over Corrado's shoulder through the glass doors of the large walk-in shower to see a pair of golden-tanned legs spread wide. A tremor worked over Ginevra's calves. He couldn't see what that hand of hers was doing between her thighs, but it was something good considering the sounds that crawled out of her throat.

"Still her favorite thing," Corrado said.

"Watching us, you mean. I fucking *know*." That was a groan because *God*, it fucked him straight up, and he loved it. "She gets off so fast, it's ... *fuck*."

"Mmhmm." He smirked against Les's mouth. "*Her turn*."

Alessio returned that by biting Corrado's jaw and muttering, "And yours."

• • •

"Kitten," Les murmured, leaning over the bed to let his fingertips drift through the stray strands of Ginevra's dark hair that had fallen over her cheek. She'd decided to take yet *another* nap. Moving the hair back over her shoulder, he then pulled the blanket down around her naked shoulder just a bit. Her eyes blinked open slowly, but he could see the tiredness there as she tried to take in her surroundings. Shit, she was in *their* bed, and she still didn't know where she was. Something wasn't right. "Time to wake up, babe. Corrado's making that—"

"Oh, *God* ..."

That was all Ginevra said before she kicked the blanket entirely off and darted off the bed. She damn near tripped over the comforter, and then her own two feet on the way to the bathroom. Alessio was too shocked and still trying to catch up to what just happened when the retching started in the bathroom.

He didn't move a muscle.

Les could do a lot. He could handle more than most.

Something he'd never been very good with, however, was vomit. Someone started puking, and he needed to be *anywhere* else because if not, he'd be the next one bent over a toilet.

"Ginevra," Les called, "do you want—"

He didn't even get his sentence finished because the noise picked up, and he was pretty sure his own gag reflex acted up just because of it.

Jesus Christ.

Five seconds after the retching started, Corrado darkened the bedroom doorway. Two voices filtered in from further down the hall.

"Is Ginny okay?" Giulia asked.

"*Ew*," Greta mumbled.

He couldn't see the girls, but then again … they learned a while back *not* to approach the bedroom but especially if the doors were open. It was as much a respect thing as it was about their privacy. He appreciated it.

Ginny probably did too at the moment.

Corrado gave Les a look, and he only shrugged back. He hated feeling helpless, but he could not go into that bathroom unless Corrado wanted to clean Alessio's vomit, too.

"You good?"

Les made a face. "If I smell—"

"*Fuck that Chinese food you brought home, Les. I knew that fish smelled bad.*"

Ginevra's cursing from the bathroom had him cringing. "Sorry."

Was it the food, though?

Because the rest of them were fine.

Corrado headed for the bathroom.

Alessio waited just long enough to hear Corrado soothing Ginny before the retching started all over again. And that was his cue to get out of there.

Perhaps to call a doctor.

Who knew?

4.

Ginevra

ACROSS the desk, the ob-gyn looked up from the folder with a smile and a nod.

"That's it?" Ginevra asked.

The doctor turned her attention to Giulia who sat beside Ginevra, waiting. "Yes, I would say that's it. I understand why she wanted to go with something like an IUD, but frankly, I feel she's a bit too young for that. The implant will work just as well, and we'll be able to have more checkups with her throughout the year while she begins her first birth control."

"So, a needle," Giulia muttered.

Ginevra did her best not to laugh, but she couldn't hide the grin when she turned on her sister. "Listen, a needle is *far* better than having an IUD put in."

"*You're* getting an IUD, Ginny."

"I'm also in my twenties, sexually active with two partners on a regular basis who are not involved with other people but each other, and I have been through the gamut of different hormonal birth control before we settled on this one. It is a better choice."

"But—"

"For *me*," she interjected quickly so Giulia wouldn't argue the point further. She wanted it clear. The two of them were not the same. She was happy her sister felt safe and comfortable coming to her to ask for proper birth control at her age because she knew her sister would be able to get it done and wouldn't make it into a *thing*. "But for you, the doctor thinks something else is a better option, so that's what we're going to go with."

"Right," the gyno replied. "And if this ends up being troublesome for whatever reason, we can discuss different options, Giulia."

The teenager beside Ginevra sighed.

What was new there?

"Condoms should still be used because this might prevent unwanted pregnancy," the doctor added, "but it does nothing for nasty things like STIs and STDs."

"Thanks for that." Guilia made a face. "I'll keep it in mind."

"You should. If you think a needle is uncomfortable, imagine a genital herpes outbreak. I have pictures if you'd like to—"

"No, that's fine," her sister rushed to say. "Perfectly good, yes. I'm good."

"Keep the pictures on hand," Ginevra said to the doctor, "just in case we need to revisit."

"Literally horrible. You really are."

"No, I just ... you know what, yeah. I am."

Guilia made a face. "Les rubs off on you too much."

Well, Ginevra wasn't about to deny that. She also wouldn't say she disliked it, either.

"I will have my assistant get the implant ready," the gyno said, bringing them back to their other conversation. "And then you ladies can be on your way." As she reached for the phone on the desk, she asked Ginevra, "How did that infection settle, anyway? The last time you were in here when we agreed on the change from the shot to the IUD, you were still on antibiotics, right?"

"It went from my ear to my throat, and now to my stomach, I think."

The woman didn't grab the phone. "Sorry?"

Ginevra didn't want to worry the doctor. After nearly four weeks of antibiotics—thank God she was done with them now and had been for a bit—she expected her stomach to begin to revolt. She had never been one who could handle long rounds of medication, but especially not the kind that made her feel like if she didn't sleep eighteen hours a day, she couldn't even walk.

Besides, she had more than enough people worrying about her between Corrado, Alessio, her sisters, and even Siena. No doubt, when she met up with Greta and Siena later in the day, *they* would ask her how she was feeling. And when she got home, *Corrado* would ask her how she was feeling. Then, Les would call later after he was done with The League and ask the same question.

Her stomach would settle soon.

Surely.

"It's nothing," Ginevra assured.

The doctor raised her brow. "Is it?"

"My stomach is upset once in a while. It's not constant, and once it happens, I am usually good for the rest of the day. I'm more concerned about the fact that I'm still sleeping fourteen hours or more a day and feeling like it's only five hours."

"Breast tenderness?"

What did that have anything to do with it?

"Not really," Ginevra said.

"But …"

"In the evenings, sometimes."

"Has your period resumed?" the doctor asked. "We were waiting for your cycle to come back after stopping the shot before I put in the IUD. You had that infection, so I hadn't bothered to ask when I saw you the second time, but has it?"

Ginevra didn't really have to think about it. "No, it hasn't."

The doctor kept staring at her. So did her sister beside her. Ginevra was starting to feel like the two of them might know something *she* did not, and she didn't like that a bit.

"What?" she asked.

The woman across the desk smiled faintly. "Is there a chance you might be pregnant?"

"*Oh.*"

Giulia dragged the word out like she was watching a

whole show. Ginevra did her best to ignore the teenager because they were always rude little shits. Even when they weren't trying to be.

"I ..." It took her a second, and then two. Finally, she managed to tell the doctor, "I'm not sure."

No, she knew it absolutely *was* a possibility. She hadn't used backup methods with Les or Corrado after stopping the shot. Being sick, there had only been a couple of times when she even felt well enough to have sex between all the times when the boys were running back and forth between New York and Vegas, so it really hadn't been a thought in her mind to begin with.

Not that either of them complained or said a thing about it to her. They'd told her once that they could take care of themselves. They knew how to get what they wanted from each other, and they did exactly that. Usually, she was the lucky bitch that got to watch while they did exactly that, too.

Not the time, Ginny.

"Should we do a pregnancy test before you leave the office while we wait for Giulia to have her implant done?" the doctor asked. "All it's going to take is a bit of urine in a cup, and I will have the results in less than seven minutes, Ginevra."

Beside her, Giulia's fingers flew over the screen of her phone, typing away a text.

"We probably should," Ginevra replied.

Her sister let out an excited screech. "Oh, my God, Greta is going to *die*."

"Do not text the boys *anything*, Giulia."

Her sister glanced up as serious as could be in a blink. "I wouldn't."

If she was pregnant—and that made *a lot* of sense now that she had a moment to think about it all—Ginevra had to tell them. *Together*. At the same time. As difficult as that might be considering how hectic their lives were at the moment.

THE FIRSTS

None of that mattered.
She would make it work.
She had to.

5.

Corrado

THE keys to Corrado's newest toy—a candy apple red Maserati—fell from his hand to the glass bowl Ginevra had set on a decorative table just beyond the brownstone's front door. The cling-clang of the keys settling into the glass had him smiling for a reason he hadn't expected, but then again, that could also be because of the man on the phone.

"Did you *attempt* to make friends today?" his father asked.

"If what you mean to ask," he returned, "is if Andino Marcello was any easier to deal with today during lunch, then the answer is *no*."

Gian chuckled. "One might think the two of you would get along considering how alike you are. Bad moods, attitudes, and all."

"One *might* think that. One would also be wrong, Papa."

"I appreciate you trying."

Corrado sighed as he shrugged off his jacket and kept the cell phone balanced between his shoulder and ear all at the same time. A feat, really. "Water under the bridge, anyway. That's what the two of us decided, and he's good with that. We will not, however, be having weekly get-togethers, and I don't think I'll join him at his dinner table. Ginevra, however …"

"Hmm, what about her?"

It took *everything* for Corrado not to scowl, but after he hung his blazer on a waiting hook and turned, he found he was still doing exactly that when he faced his reflection in a mirror across the entry hallway.

"She's made friends with Andino's wife, Haven. I blame that on Valeria, though. And Siena Marcello—John

22

Marcello's wife."

"So, essentially you will all have to make nice whether you want to or not because the wives have deemed it so."

"Why do you sound smug?" Corrado asked.

"Wives have a way of ... well, you'll understand."

"Technically, Ginevra isn't—"

"They know what she is to you and Alessio. It is the same, even if a paper doesn't say so."

Right.

"You're home now?" his father asked just as fast.

"Just got home. I was thinking ... well, it feels nostalgic for some reason. I was remembering how you always came home and dropped your keys into the candy bowl Ma had at the door. Every day. Never failed."

He swore he could feel his father's grin when Gian replied, "See, now my favorite part of that time of day was when my herd of boys came running around the corner to greet me. You all would hear the metal hitting the glass— not even the door closing. I could hear the sounds of your feet hitting the floors all the way across the mansion."

"Oh?"

"Nothing felt quite like that. Someday, you'll know, too."

Would he?

Corrado didn't know about that considering kids had never been a topic of discussion between him, Les, or Ginevra. It wasn't that he didn't want children, but rather that he didn't ever sit down and actually think about it.

"You went quiet," his father said. "My apologies if I overstep—"

"You didn't," Corrado assured. "But I smell something good coming from the kitchen, and I should make my way there, I think."

He wasn't lying.

Ginevra must be cooking *something.* It smelled rich and full of spices. Already, his mouth watered because *God ...* that woman could cook like it was nobody's business. If there was anything Corrado missed the most about living at home with his parents, it was his mother's cooking. Except now, he only had to come to *his* home for a good meal, a great man, and a perfect woman.

"Don't let my offhanded remark make you get in a headspace about something like *babies*, *figlio*," Gian said on the phone. "I was just talking to talk."

"It didn't. I want kids. Right now, I want to eat more than I want that, though."

His father chuckled. "Fine. And continue to make nice with the Marcellos, Corrado. Because goddammit, if you're going to live in New York, you need to play by *their* rules. That is the end of it."

"You wanna tell Les that, too?"

"Everyone likes Alessio. When he *tries*."

"Yeah, well …"

"Say hello to Ginevra for me. Les is where …?"

"Back in Vegas as of a couple of days ago," Corrado explained. "He had to head back for the new recruit they're training, apparently."

"You don't sound happy about that."

"I like it better when we're *all* home."

"I suppose you should work on making that happen, then, son."

Point taken.

• • •

"This is enough food to feed a small army."

Corrado's grin blew into a full-blown smile when Ginevra turned around at the kitchen island to face him. Standing in the entryway, he gave the spread on the counters a look and then passed the same to her.

"Something I missed?" he asked.

Ginevra shrugged. "I kind of … invited Siena and John to have dinner with us and the girls tonight."

He might have been annoyed by that, if only because

Johnathan Marcello was *best friends* and a cousin to Andino Marcello, but the excitement in Ginevra's eyes kept him quiet. His father was right—wives, or their women, rather—just had a way of bringing people together in this life whether they wanted to be or not.

Including his woman.

"Les will be sad he missed out," Corrado said.

Or entirely too happy, the bastard.

"No worries," Ginevra said, turning back to her work of rolling dough on the counter, "because we're going to make this a regular thing. I'm sure he'll have plenty of opportunities to join in."

"Careful. We don't play nice with others very well."

She shot him a look over her shoulder. It warned him, satisfied, and said she was amused all at the same time. "I suggest you learn, then."

Damn.

"Lucky we love you, woman."

Ginevra's laughter had Corrado crossing the kitchen in a blink before he even properly understood what he was doing. He caught her around the waist with his arm, and pulled her into his chest. He cared little that her flour-dusted hands left handprints on his black dress shirt. How could he care about that when she tipped her head back on his shoulder and reached up to press a kiss to the underside of his jaw.

Like she missed him.

God knew he missed her, too.

Always.

For a moment, the two of them stayed like that. Tucked together, lost to the silence of the house and the smells in the kitchen. Happy being close.

"Les needs to come back," Corrado muttered against the top of Ginevra's hair.

She nodded. "He does."

Spinning her around so her back faced the kitchen island, his hand found her jaw, and he tipped her head up.

Lowering his own, he took the kiss from her that he'd been waiting for all goddamn day. There was no give to her kiss—not when he took everything from it.

"*Missed you.*"

Ginevra smiled against the slowing of his lips against her own. "You better."

He chuckled. "Mmm, and hey, you went to the doctor today, right?"

"With my sister."

"*And?*"

She stared up at him, happy as could be. "You and Les worry too much. People get sick. It happens."

Corrado didn't deny that, but it told him nothing. "But what about you?"

"All is good. Normal."

"You're sure?"

"Yep."

She popped her *p*.

Corrado just laughed. "So, how long do we have before this dinner gets started? Or until the girls get back home?"

He didn't hide the suggestion at all.

"A bit. The girls are coming with Siena and John."

"Does *long enough* mean I could put you up on this counter and get your thighs wide for me? Because if I am going to have to play nice with Johnathan tonight, I need a reason to keep smiling while he's here."

A sweet heat crawled up Ginevra's cheeks. "I am *cooking* on this counter."

"Table is free."

"The table is where we will all eat."

"Yeah, us too, but you know what we did on that with Les the night before he left, right?"

Ginevra blew out a slow breath. "*Ten minutes.* That's what you've got. They might not get here for an hour or more, but I have things to do."

"Oh, you know how I love a challenge, kitten."

6.

Ginevra

"GUESS what?"

Alessio's dark tenor had Ginevra smiling in a way she knew was entirely inappropriate considering who her companion was that walked down a Manhattan street with her at the moment. They were supposed to be shopping, but she had wanted to take a walk first. Mostly the drive made her nauseous, which was exactly why she currently had a ginger sucker in one hand while she held her phone with the other.

The sucker was disgusting.

It *did* help the sick feeling.

"What?" she asked Les.

Cara passed her a look, raising a brow because *maybe* she had heard the way Ginevra's voice dared to raise a bit with her curiosity. If there was anything to know about Corrado's mother that was most important, it was that she loved her family. *All of them.*

It didn't matter if it was her sons, husband, one of the brothers' wives, or even Ginevra who really wasn't ... well, she wasn't an *official* Guzzi. Then again, neither was Les. None of that made a single difference to Cara.

She loved them all.

In fact, she often made time to come to New York just to spend time with Ginevra and Les, separately and together. As far as she understood, Cara did that with all her son's spouses. Whatever they enjoyed, she made time to do it with them.

"Say hello for me," Cara mouthed.

Ginevra nodded. "Cara says hello, Les."

"We need to visit."

"We do."

27

"Say hello back for me," he said.

"Of course."

Ginevra relayed the message, but quickly went back to her call when Cara noticed a flower vendor across the street. With a wave and a nod in that direction, Ginevra gave her a shrug and a smile to say it was okay if she left her side for a moment.

She went back to her conversation with Les.

"So, what am I trying to guess again?" she asked.

Alessio laughed huskily. "I'll be home in a few days— for at least a few months, by the way."

"*Oh?*"

"And then I'm only coming back for a few days to settle some stuff. We're taking time off."

"By *we're* do you also mean—"

"Corrado, too. We've been working on it."

Huh.

For a brief moment, Ginevra said nothing because she just wanted to take that information in. She knew the boys wanted to be more permanent with her in New York, but it took a lot for them to even get a couple weeks at a time with her. The League always had something on the go that one, or both, needed to handle. She accepted that was just a part of their life together, and since she wanted them … well, this was a sacrifice she needed to make.

"I should probably start finalizing rooms for the brownstone with the designer, then," Ginevra said. "If we're all going to be there."

"Don't forget the reading nook in the bedroom. It's the only thing I wanted."

Ginevra laughed. "Well …"

"We'll get back to it. Seems like we have time. Or we will."

"Soon," she said.

"Soon," he echoed.

"I miss you, Les."

"Yeah, I know. Love you, huh?"

"More than the moon and the stars."

It was true.

Nothing about her life would be the same because of these men. Ginevra was fine with that.

• • •

"So, Les will be coming home soon, then?"

"Seems so," Ginevra replied, pushing another dress aside on the hanger to look at another. None of them really screamed *Sunday services appropriate,* but she was determined to find something new. Same as Cara. "And he said something about Corrado getting time off, too. I won't complain about any of it, let me say."

"I bet. My favorite part of the day was when we were all home. As loud and busy as it was ... none of it mattered when all my boys were in the house and their father was home, too. I miss those days."

"Does the mansion seem ... empty now?"

"Sometimes," Cara admitted, "but someone is always coming or going and that keeps me more than busy enough not to think on it for too long."

She stuck the sucker back in her mouth that had been her second companion all morning and mumbled, "Ah."

"You know," Cara said, peering over the rack of hanging dresses to meet Ginevra's stare, "I can't say I have ever seen you walk around with a sucker in your hand all day."

Ginevra pulled the ginger sucker from her mouth with a *pop* and a sheepish smile. "Sorry—not very appropriate, is it?"

Cara laughed and waved it off. "Just thought it was a new thing."

"It is."

Then, the woman on the other side of the rack gave the sucker another look. She hadn't paid it much mind earlier in the day as they moved from one boutique to the next looking for the perfect hat to go with Cara's Sunday dress she planned to wear to church.

"Is that ... a ginger sucker? I swear I can't forget that smell."

Ginevra tried to shrug it off. "Yeah, I picked some up just to try."

"I used those when I was pregnant with the twins. It helped to keep the nausea at bay, but it did nothing for the morning sickness. Can't imagine why anyone would want to just suck on one of those like they're actually *good*."

Not knowing what to say, Ginevra opted to say nothing at all. That probably wasn't the right thing to do considering her silence had Cara staring at her longer and harder than before. All at once, the woman's eyes widened before her gaze darted back and forth between the sucker Ginevra held and her face.

"Are you ... are you *pregnant*?" Cara asked.

She was not a good liar.

At all.

"I—"

"You don't have to tell me. Maybe I shouldn't have asked. I'm sorry. Let's pretend like I didn't say anything."

"I am," Ginevra blurted out, "but I haven't told the boys yet. I wanted to do it when we're all together, but that's hard when you know, they're gone one right after the other. And how do I tell them that anyway? I don't know which of them is the fath—"

"Is that going to matter?"

Ginevra really didn't have to think about it. This thing between her, Corrado and Alessio had never been about the separate relationships. It was the life they made together. "No, it won't. How do I tell them, though?"

Cara smiled softly. "Well, that's part of the wonder. You can tell them however you want. But *me* ... well, I am telling my husband as soon as he picks up his phone."

To make her point, Cara even pulled out her phone and started dialing.

"Make sure he doesn't tell anyone else!"

Cara grinned as she put the phone to her ear. "Oh, we won't. No worries." Then, Gian must have finally answered his phone because Cara turned her back to Ginevra as she started shouting, "Gian! Gian, guess what I know that you don't know ... no, Corrado didn't start a war with the Marcellos—would you stop worrying about that, *God*. Listen, this is important. W*e're going to have a grandbaby*!"

7.

Alessio

"THAT'LL be—"

Alessio tossed a fifty-dollar bill over the driver's shoulder and stepped out of the back of the taxi as the man mumbled his thanks. He could have called someone to pick him up, or even drove one of their many cars still in storage in Vegas home, but he didn't.

The flight was faster.

He'd already been away long enough.

The cab pulled away from the curb in front of the brownstone, but Alessio didn't move. He took in the twisted metal gate that opened to a pathway leading to the home. The few potted plants and hanging flowers Ginevra hung up were new. They must have come after he left the last time, and he just … wanted to take it all in.

He was home.

Where he belonged.

Les wouldn't be leaving *anytime* soon.

Dragging in a lungful of air that tasted *nothing* like Vegas, he pulled out his phone as he opened the gate to see a text from both Dare and Cree. One hoped he arrived safely— the other demanded he call to let them know he got there fine.

Both had him smiling.

He would call.

Later.

Dare and Cree would understand.

Right now, Les had more important things on his mind. Like the man and the woman waiting for him inside that brownstone. They knew the time of his flight, and when he should be arriving in New York, but they didn't know when he was actually getting to their home.

Well, here he was.

He found the front door unlocked, and the familiar noise floating down the hallway that greeted him had Les smiling wider than ever.

"See, you can't even beat me at *Tetris*, Corrado. You really need to stop."

"I'll find a damn game I can win," he heard his other lover mutter.

Les took in the entryway and the fact it was finally decorated. Hooks lined the walls with coats and sweaters hanging from each one. A large mosaic-designed vase sat near the side of a decorative table in the hallway filled with umbrellas. Shoes lined the floor near the wall. A long carpet kept the floors clean where people had to take off their shoes.

Even the walls had things hanging from it.

Photos.

Art.

A mirror.

"Let's go another round," Corrado said, drawing Alessio's attention back down the hall again as he set his bag down. Shrugging off his coat, he listened as the two continued their battle of wills about gaming. It never failed to amuse him how seriously they both took their games, and at the same time, it felt *just* like home to hear them going on about it. "At least give me a chance to save my pride."

Ginny scoffed. "*What* pride?"

Alessio made quick work of kicking off his shoes, but he kept his leather jacket on. Heading down the hallway, he turned the corner at the end to enter the living room where he found Corrado and Ginevra sitting on opposite ends of the couch with a game of Tetris flashing on the television.

"His *pride*, Ginny. The thing that's always haunted him no matter what he does," Alessio said.

All at once, two pairs of eyes turned on Alessio. Their

smiles matched his own, and the need growing in his chest had him crossing the floor before he could think better of it. He made it to the back of the couch when Ginevra reached out a hand for him. He took it with his own, weaving their fingers together as he leaned down to grab Corrado's jaw with his other.

"Someone would have come to pick you up," she told him.

Corrado arched a brow. "What she said."

"I know," he replied simply.

Alessio bent down, turning Corrado's face at the same time to take a kiss from him. He lingered just long enough to feel the way Corrado let him find the taste he wanted before he let him go. Then, Les moved to Ginevra to do the same. Her sweet little hum against his kiss had him feeling like home was *exactly* where his heart was.

It's right where he wanted to stay, too.

Forever.

Alessio didn't bother to round the couch to sit down. That wasn't really his style, anyway. No, he simply jumped over the back and landed right in the middle between Corrado and Ginevra. Their loud—but *fake*—complaints settled once he was seated. One of his arms snaked over the back of the couch behind Ginevra, so he could play with the softness of her hair while his other landed tight to Corrado's thigh.

All over again, he felt good.

Happy.

Right again.

There was something about coming home that filled a void in Alessio's chest. Maybe it was because he'd never really had what one might consider a traditional or proper home. Even the penthouse in Vegas he shared with Corrado had been more like a hideaway for the two of them than a home.

Now that he had been away from the place he called home more often than he was here, he tended to notice the long stretches of time far more. He didn't want to be gone.

He wanted to be home.

"Someone is getting their ass beat again, yeah?" he asked.

"Fuck off," Corrado muttered. "How is she this good?"

Ginevra only grinned.

"How was the flight?"

Les shrugged in answer to Corrado. "Decent. Same as it usually is."

"So, cramped, long, and loud."

"Basically."

Ginevra waved at the television. "Are we beating Corrado's ass again, or what?"

Laughter filled up the living room. The game started quickly, and while he watched the split screen on the television and the blocks coming down one after the other for the two people on either side of him to make lines with, Alessio had another thought.

"So, if the entryway is all decorated, does that mean the reading nook is also finished?"

"Oh, no," Ginevra said, never once looking away from the game, "that's a surprise."

Alessio tipped his head to the side, giving Corrado a look. His lover only shrugged back clearly not having an answer to his unspoken question.

That was fine.

Les liked surprises.

Mostly.

8.

Corrado

"HAVE you ever thought that maybe Ginny would want to have her stuff in here with ours?" Alessio asked.

Turning away from the hanging bag where he put his suits that needed to be dry-cleaned, Corrado nodded. "I have."

"And yet, it's only our things in this walk-in closet."

"Because this is what we do, Les. Every morning. Every night."

Corrado almost smiled at the way Alessio had to take a second to consider what he said. He wasn't lying. He and Les always got ready for their day or night *together*. Ginevra preferred to do those things separately, and alone in her own space.

Then, Corrado tipped his chin toward the doorway. "Besides, the door's always open. She knows that."

"Right. Did Dare call?"

"Gave me the okay on the time off, actually."

"Good," Les murmured. "He owes us both."

"That was not how he put it to me."

Alessio's dark chuckles came close to the back of Corrado's neck when he turned to finish zipping up the garment bag. Just as fast, he felt Les's hot mouth find the skin of his bare shoulder blade while the side of his hand brushed along Corrado's.

Soft touches.

Quiet moments.

Amid everything else that had changed in their life, and after all Corrado had done to them that could have ruined what he and Alessio shared together … well, at the end of the day, they were still the same.

And he liked that just fine.

"Missed you," Les murmured against Corrado's shoulder.

"More than you know."

"Turn the heat up for Ginny, yeah?"

Corrado chuckled as he turned around, cocking a brow all the while. "She still won't sleep under blankets."

"Yeah, well … I think she's warm enough between the two of us, that's all."

"Stop talking about me in there, I hear you!"

Ginevra's teasing yell from outside the walk-in closet had Alessio winking at Corrado. The asshole looked so pleased with himself—or maybe it was just because he was finally home—that Corrado couldn't help but kiss him.

He didn't linger.

Couldn't.

Not if he wanted to leave this closet because as soon as he got a taste of Les, well, he'd be fucked. A lot like he was whenever he got his mouth on Ginevra and had five minutes on his hands to waste.

"Setting this up to be a good night, yeah?" Corrado asked over his shoulder as he headed for the door leading back to the bedroom.

Alessio grinned, flashing his teeth and everything. He went from playful to sinful in a fucking *blink*. "You know it."

"Know what?" Ginevra, already in the middle of the bed with a binder in her hands, glanced up with a curious glint. "Hmm?"

"Just Les and his incessant need to test my self-control every chance he gets."

"I don't need to test *anything*. We all know what your self-control is like, thank you."

Ginevra glanced up, staring at the ceiling before she just as quickly went back to whatever was in that binder with a nod. "He's not wrong."

"See," Alessio said.

Smug as fuck.

Corrado smirked. "Yeah, well …"

"Nobody's complaining," Ginevra added.

"Exactly."

Alessio gave Corrado another one of those winks as he headed for the small attached enclave of their master bedroom that was supposed to be for the reading nook he'd wanted. Really, it was the only thing he asked to be done in the entire house. He knew there would be a gym—Corrado was the one who demanded that. The office would also double as a library because they all liked that idea.

The reading nook, though …

"I really wanted this," Alessio said, his voice muffled from where they couldn't see him inside the enclave. "Can't see what would be so important that we'd change it, honestly."

Corrado looked Ginevra's way to find she was chewing on her bottom lip while she closed the binder in her hands and set it on her lap. "He *never* whines."

"I know," she whispered. "But … it's a good surprise."

"You didn't even tell me what the change in plans were, kitten."

"I wanted you both here when I did it."

Corrado laughed, and headed for the bed. Putting both his hands at the edge, he leaned over and pressed a quick kiss to Ginevra's temple. Her pretty lips curved with the sweetest smile, and her gaze drifted to the entry of the enclave where Alessio had come back to stand.

"We're both here," he said.

"You are," she murmured.

"So," Les urged, "what happened to the reading nook?"

"I thought …" Ginevra swallowed hard, shrugging the delicate line of her shoulders under a silk camisole as Corrado stood straight, and Alessio joined him near the side of the bed. "Well, it's better suited for something else because it's right in the bedroom, there's still privacy, and we'll hear the baby as soon as they cry for us."

All at once, Corrado's heart stopped.

He was sure it did.

Beside him, Alessio made a noise.

Soft and *thick*.

Unsure and *excited*.

"What baby?" Corrado heard himself ask.

Alessio's hand found Corrado's wrist, and he grabbed tight. Tighter than he'd ever held him before, and while someone else might have thought that action wasn't a good thing, he could *feel* the other man's joy radiating. When someone spent enough time with another person who owned a part of their soul, they learned to distinguish things like that.

"The sleeping ... getting sick," Alessio said. "That's because you're—"

Corrado made a noise that time, stopping the man beside him from saying more. He didn't want *Alessio* to say it, even if they both figured it out. It was Ginevra's news, and it should be *her* who told them. She waited, after all.

He understood that now.

She waited for them.

For them to *be* a them.

All together.

The way they should be.

"You say it," Corrado told her. "Tell us like you wanted to, kitten."

She grinned.

Sexy *and* sweet.

Alessio's fingers tightened around Corrado's wrist again. "Yeah, Ginny."

Ginevra set the binder aside and moved to her knees where she rested at the side of the bed. In front of both of them. "So, that's the thing ... I'm about ten weeks preg—"

Alessio took her down to the bed first with a shout before he pinned Ginevra down and kissed every breathless laugh that fell from her lips. Corrado was *very* quick to follow.

Tucked between them with her laughter muffled, one of her hands tight around Alessio's middle while her other reached back to hook Corrado's neck, Ginevra trembled. And then he felt Les's lips find his forehead overtop her, the softest kiss.

"We're gonna have a baby," he murmured to Corrado. Then, the two of them glanced down. Ginevra stared up at both of them, her top teeth catching her bottom lip as she smiled. "We're having a baby?"

"*Yeah,*" she breathed.

They were having a *baby*.

9.

Seven months later ...

"I *can't* ... I-I can't, I just—"

"Yes, you can," Les murmured, his face clouding Ginevra's hazy vision. She did her best to focus on him and Corrado resting behind her on the bed if only because that was easier to process than the absolute *agony* ripping through her lower half. "She's right there, babe. She's got the prettiest black curls, and she wants her mom to hold her."

"One more," Corrado said in her ear. "You can do one more, Ginny."

The music she wanted played still hummed in the background of their master bedroom, but she couldn't distinguish what song was currently echoing through the speakers. Not that it mattered because the sound of her boys talking her through the hardest experience of her life to date took every ounce of her concentration.

She was grateful for them.

Needed them for this.

It was every reason why the three of them were in the *bedroom* of their home with a midwife between her legs with her fingers probing against the crowning of their baby's head because she needed *them here.* With her.

Her gyno had been great throughout the whole pregnancy. She was open-minded and didn't say half of the ignorant things a lot of others who should have known better did when it came to the pregnancy, and their life. But when it came to the hospital, the policy was *one* support person in the room, and it didn't matter how many times they explained *both* fathers had to be in the

41

room, no one would budge.

So, they found themselves here. With a midwife who worked in her gyno's office, in their bed where she felt *most* comfortable while her two boys were exactly where they wanted and needed to be, and their family filled the brownstone to wait for the birth of their daughter.

The *first* Guzzi child of her generation.

They had more than enough people who felt the need to voice their concerns. From everything to how far away a hospital was to whether or not a name was going to be put on the birth certificate. As though women hadn't been giving birth since the beginning of time and which name a baby was given at birth would make or break it all despite all their love. None of it made any difference to the three of them, though.

They knew what they wanted.

This baby was *theirs*.

What did the rest matter?

"One more," Alessio assured, "that's all."

"With the next contraction, Ginevra," the midwife agreed, "and she'll be right out into my arms and ready for you to meet her."

"You ready?" Corrado asked.

Ginevra took a moment. Just one single second to take in her surroundings and everything else. Her *men*. The one with his arms wrapped around her chest where he sat behind her. And the other on the edge of the bed with both her hands in his. They never forgot each other; she knew it. Even when it seemed like Corrado and Alessio were in entirely different worlds, all it took was a single look between them for everything to settle.

Right now, though, it was all about her.

And their *baby*.

She was sweaty.

Aching all over.

Was she ready to be a mom?

Was she ready for everything to change?

"Yeah, I'm ready," she replied, voice quaking with every word. "Let's have this baby."

Coraline Sorrento Guzzi came into the world at six-oh-two in the evening with matted black curls stuck to her little head which they quickly covered with a knitted pink cap to keep her warm. She had ten fingers, ten toes, and two hazy blue eyes that found Ginevra's the moment she was put to her mother's breast. Her daddies cried. It was too much; she didn't realize how instantaneous the overwhelming love would be for her baby until she was put in her arms.

They already had a life. Too much love to go around, really. In that moment, though, with her first breath, their daughter made them into something else.

A family.

CHRISTOPHER & VALERIA: PART 2

10.

Chris

"I can't be late!"

"You're not going to be late," Chris assured Maria as he set her up on the kitchen island. She shoved a quarter of a piece of jam toast into her mouth like it was the last thing she was going to eat for the rest of her life. Really, she was just rushing unnecessarily. Like her mother, however, he found that he couldn't tell the girl her anxieties were for nothing without causing a bigger issue. So, he opted to just do his duties and get her out the door and into his car for school. "We're not running late, Maria."

"Ten minutes later than yesterday!"

She had a point.

Frankly, Chris needed the extra ten minutes of snooze time that morning and still didn't regret hitting that button earlier. Would he need to go ten over the limit the whole way to Maria's private Catholic school?

Likely.

Still worth it.

Rounding the island so that he came behind Maria on the other side, Chris already had a brush and elastic ready. She finished destroying her toast while he pulled her long, dark black hair into the high pony she liked. A few sweeps of the brush to smooth everything down, and he easily slipped the elastic down the tail of her hair to keep it in place.

Chris checked the clock.

Two minutes.

Not bad at all.

"Come on, Daddy," Maria muttered, not even bothering to wait for Chris to come around the counter to help her down before she jumped all on her own. "We gotta go

45

now."

"Maria," he murmured, coming around the island again to stand in front of her. Well, he kneeled to be mostly eye-level with his daughter. He still thought it was ignorant and arrogant of adults to talk *over* kids when they would get far better results talking *with* them. "We're not going to be late, baby. I promise."

She let out a sigh, put one hand to her little hip, and those dark eyes of hers nailed right into his. It was only the browns of her eyes that sometimes made people pause when he introduced her as his daughter. Even those who didn't know them, or the situation of how he had come to be with Valeria and in the process, adopted her daughter as his own—unofficially, at first, and then properly on paper later.

The browns of their eyes made people wonder—was she *his*? They looked so much alike that even the gold flakes in her gaze matched his own.

Not that it mattered.

Blood didn't always make a family.

But like this, with her little hand on her hip while she stared at him as though he was being entirely ridiculous and she just couldn't believe it, Maria looked the *most* like her mother. Chris kind of loved that, too.

"Okay," Maria said, "but listen, Daddy, I finally learned how to sing the Canadian anthem *in French*, and I don't want to miss singing it with the rest of my class when they do morning notes on the speakers. So, we have to leave. Right now."

"You won't miss it."

She gave him another look, and pursed her pink lips. "Promise?"

Chris held out his pinky for her to take with his own because it was still the very best way for Maria to trust any promise he made her. "*Pinky* promise."

Maria hooked their fingers and shook on it. "I gotta go get my book bag."

"I'll meet you at the front door."

"Got it!"

She yelled that over her shoulder as she headed for the kitchen entryway, passing her oncoming mother on the way. The sparkly pink running shoes were a stark contrast to the pleated skirt, high black socks that reached her little knees, and the white shirt with a bow at the collar the school used as a uniform.

But, the kids were allowed to wear whatever shoes they wanted, and Maria always had to have something that stood out from the rest. Even if they didn't match her outfit.

"What was that all about?" Val asked, grinning as she crossed the kitchen.

Standing, Chris met his wife of almost five months—two weeks before they hit that milestone—with a smile that matched her own. Before answering her question, he dragged her close for a quick, burning kiss that he hadn't been able to get from her that morning because she'd been too busy running for the shower while he attempted to get Maria ready for school.

Life with a kid was chaotic.

Chris wouldn't change it.

Not for anything.

Slowing his kiss so that he could just enjoy the way Valeria's lips moved in tandem with his own, he pressed his forehead to hers and took a moment to have her there with him. *Present.* Safe. And entirely happy.

Also, *his.*

"Nothing," he assured her. "She just wants to get to school. I think the French tutor has helped to make her ... more comfortable, you know? So many kids in that school are bilingual, and she knows it makes her different that she can't talk like they do."

Val huffed. "Maybe they should learn *her* second language."

"I'm in the process of donating enough that they'll have

a year-round class of Spanish and a summer program. In the meantime, French will be her third language. What's wrong with that?"

"Well ..."

He gave her a look.

Val only rolled her eyes. "Thank you."

"Never thank me for loving you two, yeah?"

"I know. Still will."

Probably.

He'd still remind her that she didn't have to.

"Thanks for taking her this morning," Val added. "I can't believe they changed the time of my doctor's appointment that late last night."

"It's fine. I got it. And the doctor ... that's all standard stuff, right?"

"Just getting the IUD removed and switching to the shot once everything settles."

Chris cleared his throat. "Do you want to change birth controls, or ..."

"We need *something.*"

"Do we?"

Val stilled. "Are you asking me *not* to get a new birth control?"

"I'm saying we didn't really talk about it, and maybe I would like to. Or perhaps you would, but since we didn't take a minute to sit down and chat, neither of us know what the other wants. That's all."

"When do we have time?" she shot back, grinning.

Chris laughed. "Point taken. But I'm taking the time *now.*"

"Yeah, right now when you're late taking our daughter to school, and I have forty-five minutes to get to the city for this damn appointment. Probably not the best time, Chris."

"Maybe I'm giving you forty-five minutes to think about what *you* want, then."

"Daddy! Now we're fifteen minutes behind!"

"I'll bump the speed up to fifteen over the limit," he told Val.

She gave him a cocked brow.

He winked right back.

"Think about it, okay?" he asked.

Valeria wet her bottom lip. "I will."

"Good."

One more kiss to his wife's lips, a quick *I love you*, and he was chasing Maria's calls to hurry up before the two slipped out of the house into the cool October air. It felt like it was going to be a good day, though.

It always did with them.

11.

Valeria

"BAD traffic?"

Valeria smiled tiredly as she pulled the book bag from her wiggling daughter who was already trying to run toward the woman who asked the question. Chris's mother, Cara, waited in the middle of the large Guzzi mansion's entry in front of the winding staircases.

"Bad accident on the highway," Val explained, standing straight with a dangling, pink book bag in her hands. "Ended up sitting there for almost an hour before we could pass, and by that time—"

Cara laughed. "The highway was so backed up with cars, yeah. That drives me crazy, too. The only bad thing about living in or near a major city."

"Nanna!"

"Hey, pretty girl! Come give me some love."

Val took the chance with her daughter's distraction to set the girl's bag, shoes, and jacket aside. Across the entry, Cara greeted Maria as though she had known and loved Val's daughter for her entire life. The second after the girl asked Cara if she could be her *nonny*, though she mostly used nanna, Chris's mother took her new role seriously. Playdates, movies, special dinners, and visits every chance she could. Maria loved every single second of it.

It warmed Val's heart because it was everything her daughter hadn't even known she needed. Chris gave them an entire family. Maria had more uncles and aunts than she could keep count of between the Guzzi family and Haven's new family with the Marcellos. It also kept them busy running from one country to the next, but she wasn't about to complain, either.

Sometimes, a person didn't realize what they were

missing until they finally had it. Valeria had never been more aware of that fact until now. Not that it made a difference to how she felt—all she could ever be for what she had now was *grateful*. This life she had was only possible because of them. She would do anything to protect these people.

Always.

"Did you finally do it?" she heard Cara ask.

Maria nodded, her excitement practically filling the mansion full. "I did. I sang it *all* and didn't make one mistake."

"See, I told you. Well done, Maria."

Val smiled.

Maria had been practicing the French version of Canada's national anthem ever since she started at the new school. Over the summer, she had every single person she could singing it back to her, so she could sing along with them.

Finally, she got it.

The kid might as well have her moment.

She worked for it, after all.

"Guess what I've got to celebrate?" Cara asked.

Maria glanced over her shoulder and her eyes went wide in her joyful anticipation. Just as fast, her attention went right back to her grandmother. "*What?*"

"The special candy-coated popcorn we found the last time we went to the—"

"*Yassss!*"

Cara laughed, standing straight and giving Maria a kiss to the top of her head when the girl hugged her legs as though she might never let go. "You'll find it in the kitchen. Be careful, it's next to the teapot."

"Oh, is the tea for me?" Val asked.

"I had to do something special for you, too. Even if it is only tea, Val."

"You are special enough, Cara."

The older woman only shrugged and smiled. With one

more order for Maria to go find her treat, the girl left the grown-ups alone as she headed for the kitchen. Valeria finally took the time to take off her own coat and shoes before hanging her purse from a waiting hook near the door. Cara crossed the floor to stand close enough that she could pull Val into a hug.

"And how was *your* day?" her mother-in-law asked.

She didn't think many women were as lucky as she was to have in-laws who cared about their children's significant others as much as Cara Guzzi did. Well, even Gian was always calling to make sure Val and Maria had everything they needed whenever they might want it.

"A little uncomfortable when they pulled my IUD out, but other than that," she said, "it was pretty good."

Cara made a face. "Ouch."

"Yeah, well … it needed to be done. I knew when I had the stupid thing put in that at some point in time, it was going to have to come back *out*. Maybe if they were kinder about the fact it hurts, women wouldn't feel so traumatized after the process."

"Agreed," Cara murmured. "But very little about women's reproductive health is about making us comfortable, or so I have learned over time. Especially if you get an older man as a doctor—bonus points if he has white hair and opinions about things that are none of his goddamn concern."

Wasn't that the truth?

"The doctor gave me orders to come back for the shot after my first cycle resumed. That could take a couple of weeks or a month. Who knows?"

Everything was up in the air.

Cara clearly heard the *off* tone because she raised an eyebrow at Val, saying, "Did I miss something?"

Val took a second to think if she wanted to respond honestly to Cara's question, or just brush it off because it was something personal between her and Chris. Honestly, though, she needed someone to talk to. And not someone who was currently pregnant—like Ginevra, or Haven—because they were biased.

"I never thought I wanted more kids after Maria," Valeria said quietly, "but I think that was more because of my circumstances and, you know, how she came along to be mine."

"And now?"

Valeria laughed lightly. "Chris said something to me this morning as I was getting ready and he was leaving—to think about it. Now, that's all I've done all day. I feel like I've talked myself in a million circles. How do you know if you're ready for a child?"

"You have *a* child, Val."

"Another child, then."

Cara gave her a look. "Or do you mean a child you willingly create."

"I never use those words for my daughter. I will never call her a product of—I love her, Cara. And I know my life now isn't anything like what it used to be."

"But that doesn't change the trauma, or what used to be. And nobody—including my son—expects you to wake up one day and forget everything that came before him. I promise you that."

"Maybe I worry, too."

"About what?"

"That I'll feel differently this time around ... or *more*. Maybe that the glass ceiling over my head will shatter. I don't know. Everything?"

Cara reached out and cupped Valeria's cheek with a soft touch that only a mother could have. She patted her with the same kindness, saying, "And no matter what, you're a wonderful mother. She knows that—we all know that. The rest is all up to you, Val."

Yeah. She was right.

"After our tea," Val said, "would you mind watching Maria for the night? I think I kind of left Chris hanging even if he just said for me to think about it ... I don't want him to assume that I don't have an answer for him."

Because she did. He was right. She'd just needed to think about it.

"Not a problem at all," Cara assured.

12.

"TEN percent," Kevin, a more recent addition to their Capos, offered.

Chris scoffed. "You're being fucking offensive to my sensibilities."

"Thought you Guzzis didn't *have* sensibilities?"

"Only when it comes to our money."

"Fine. *Fifteen.*"

Chris gave the man a look. "Absolutely not."

"Christopher, be reasonable. This new racket will bring in two-point-two million *yearly*. I made this deal a reality. Your father is only going to have to sit back and *collect*. Surely, just this once, we can lessen the tribute percentage for this cash flow."

"How do you think *any* of our money is made?" Chris asked, leaning back in the dining chair so he could get a good look at the restaurant floor behind the other man. He always sat with his back towards a wall without windows, never failed. He knew better than to be the fool with his back to a room of people he wasn't sure he could trust. "Men like you, and a lot of others like you, go out and make *deals*. Or widen your illegal businesses through our other lines of power and control. This is how the mafia works, Kevin."

"Yes, but—"

"And do you know what you get in return for your hard work and monthly tribute to our family?"

The man across the table sighed heavily. "No, but I am sure you're going to tell me."

"Of course. This is a learning opportunity for you, and I don't want to waste it."

"No need to be patronizing."

Wrong.

It was always time for that.

There was a reason the Guzzis remained on top, and untouched. Chris had zero qualms with reminding the man across from him exactly what that reason happened to be. Kevin was new to his capo seat having taken it over after an older capo finally retired his position and specifically vouched for the man he'd mentored for years. Given Gian and the rest of the Guzzi men knew Kevin quite well and had worked with him at various points in his career over the years in their Cosa Nostra, there hadn't been any objections to his new place.

There still wouldn't be.

If the man shut his damn mouth.

"So," Chris said, smiling a bit at the sight of a familiar woman nearing the windows of the restaurant, "allow me to make this quick because that right there is my wife coming in to see me. Since I wasn't expecting her, she always makes my moods better, and I'm about over this conversation, listen closely, Kevin."

The Capo said nothing.

Chris figured ... *points to your favor, man.*

"You see, this is how it has always worked. And in return for the money you make us, we offer you protection, respect, and a safe way to do your illegal business, Kevin. If for some reason you want the status quo to change because you think you deserve more for doing the same work better men have been doing for us for years, then I suggest," Chris said, standing from the table and downing what was rest of his glass of whiskey at the same time, "that you make a choice to move on from our *famiglia*, or even, start out on your own."

The man's expression remained blank.

Chris set the glass down to the table, and pulled his jacket from the back of the chair he'd been using to slip it on at the same time that he added, "Although, do keep in mind with those actions also come consequences. Step out to someone else that isn't an ally, and we'll consider that a threat. Start out on your own, and we'll see you as competition to remove."

"Chris—"

"If you have something that is not an apology, then I suggest you keep your mouth shut as you've said more than enough to me. Thirty percent. That is the tribute. That will *remain* the tribute to my father for our business. Is that understood?"

Across the restaurant, Valeria finally laid eyes on Chris. She lifted a hand, smiled and waved. He did the same back, but his gaze quickly cut down to the man still sitting at the table while he waited patiently for an answer.

"My apologies," Kevin muttered. "I understand how this *famiglia* works, Christopher."

"Good. Keep it in mind. We'll all be better for it."

With his bit said, Chris left the table while he fixed the two buttons at the front of his blazer through their proper slits. He made his way toward his wife and enjoyed the growing smile on her face. He hadn't expected to see her for hours—not until he made his way back home after his daily business was done.

As a Capo, and one that had a heavy hand in a lot of duties directly for his father and brothers … well, his days sometimes felt never-ending.

This was a nice surprise.

"I'm not dressed for this place, am I?" Val asked when he was near enough to hear her.

Chris laughed. "I own the damn place, who cares how you fucking look? Besides, you look just *fine*, babe."

And she did in her skinny jeans and a silk blouse. Never looked better. Then again, she always looked good to him. His walking wet dream with all those curves, and her brown skin that tasted of salt and sin when she was under him.

Yeah.

Perfect.

"Come here," he said, arms already open.

The second she was in his hold, he kissed her. A long, lingering kiss. One that had their lips moving in tandem, the familiar rhythm soothing and yet still hot enough to make him harden beneath his slacks.

"How was the doctor?" he asked.

Val made a face. "About as you'd expect. At least, the cramping stopped and so did the spotting. Which means my night won't be ruined. Did I interrupt something?"

"Pardon?"

She pointed over his shoulder.

Chris didn't bother to look back. "Of course not. You could never interrupt."

And the mafia?

It never touched his wife.

Chris made sure of it.

"Can I tell you something?" Val asked.

He smiled. "Always. Anything."

"Sometimes, I still think all of this is a dream. Even though I know it isn't and this is very much our happily ever after, I still sometimes worry I'm going to wake up and everything is going to change for me, or you … or us."

"Never."

It was a promise.

He always kept those.

Valeria nodded, still locking onto his gaze and holding tight. "So, I did what you said. I thought about everything. Ended up thinking about it long after I had my IUD taken out and was told it would be a while before I could even get the shot."

"Oh?"

"If everything changes, Chris, I want it to be because *I* chose for it to be different."

"Everything is always your choice with me, Val. Even something like this."

"A baby. *Say it.*"

Chris grinned, unashamed. "Yes, a *baby.*"

"I'm not going to have the shot."

His hold on her tightened a bit. "Is that so?"

"Seems that way."

Chris dragged in a quick breath. "Huh."

"And just because, your mom is watching Maria tonight, so we have the house to ourselves whenever you get home."

"Right now, you mean."

Valeria laughed. "No, just finish your business. I thought maybe I left you hanging this morning, and I didn't want you going one more minute wondering. I'm fine, and I will be waiting at home as I always am whenever you finish your work."

"I am finished, Val. Nothing is more important than you."

And that would forever be the case.

He'd make sure of it.

Pulling her in close, he wrapped his arms around her the same way she did to him. He found the soft, sweet-tasting skin of her neck with a kiss, murmuring, "Let's go home, babe."

13.

Valeria

IT was unusual for their home to be so quiet that they could hear the music floating out of the stereo system set up in Chris's office. The noise he liked to constantly keep going because he swore that was how he focused the best.

Valeria didn't argue it.

To each their own.

Usually, the house had some kind of noise between them, Maria's three kittens, someone who was always coming in and out, or even her and Chris. Unless their daughter was sleeping or she wasn't home—like now—the house had life.

All the lights were dimmed.

Soft music floated through.

Chris watched Val from where he leaned against the kitchen table while she drank her glass of wine, savoring the flavors that reminded her of Abril's favorite bottle back in Mexico. She wasn't *really* a wine fan, but at the same time, it allowed her a bit of nostalgia that didn't also leave her feeling guilty, or worse, traumatized like everything else about her past did.

Tipping the glass up to her lips, she grinned a bit when Chris tilted his head to the side. "I should enjoy this one more," she told him, "because I plan for it to be my last for a while."

His lips split with the sexiest smirk. "Oh?"

She shrugged. "Better safe than sorry, I guess."

"True."

Pushing away from the table, Chris strode across the kitchen floor with determined, purposeful steps. Each one that he took brought him closer and closer for Valeria. She swore her heart felt every single one of them, too.

God.

She loved this man.

He would never know how much.

She didn't know the words to say.

Valeria managed to empty what little wine was left in her glass before Chris caught it with his own hand. He set it to the countertop behind her while the pad of his thumb came up to stroke her bottom lip with a touch that had shivers racing straight down her spine.

Yes.

It was going to be a damn good night.

She could tell already.

He moved in a little closer, the sway of his body and sensual curve of his lips only adding to his appeal when he murmured, "Do you hear the music?"

"It should be illegal to look like you do in a pair of slacks with a dress shirt rolled up to your elbows."

Chris chuckled. "But what about the music?"

"Yes, I hear it."

The current song just happened to be something sexier and fast paced. A popular club song that had people moving close to grind and sway to the beat together.

"Dance with me," he said, putting his hand out palm up for her to take.

This time, it wasn't a request.

Val wouldn't deny him.

Couldn't.

Why would she when he looked like he did waiting for her? The second her palm met his, Chris's fingers tightened around hers, and he pulled her away from the counter. Somehow, it seemed like the music became louder when he spun her to him. Her chest molded against his, and her palm came up to rest between them while her fingernails dug just a little into his chest.

She wanted him to feel that heat, too. The same heat he awoke in her every single time he touched her. Every morning he woke her up by being between her thighs.

Each husky call of her name.

All of him.

She never thought to ask where Chris learned to dance like he knew exactly how to move his body to each and every song played on the radio, but the man did. The way he could move his hips in time with hers while keeping her close enough that could feel every one of her racing heartbeats while his mouth was attacking her neck made her weak in the knees every single time.

Then again, everything this man did made her feel that way. From the grins on his face in the mornings to the way he took his time stripping her naked in the kitchen after their dance before lifting her up to the counter and stepping between her thighs.

He stroked her awake.

With a dance.

Then a strip.

A teasing touch.

A *promising kiss*.

"*God*, I love you," he breathed into their kiss.

"I love you more than you will ever know, Chris."

Because she'd not yet found the right way to tell him. God knew she tried time and time again, yet each time she ended up with the same line: *I love you.*

That seemed to suit him just fine.

Cool air whispered over her naked skin. Yet, all she seemed to be was *hot*.

Chris made it *so much better* when he slid inside her, stretching her wide and filling her full with one thrust that took her straight up to heaven.

All she asked for then was *more*.

He gave her that, too.

14.

One month later ...

"NO, we'll figure something out soon, Haven," Val said. "Yeah, I promise. What's happening over there, anyway?"

Chris came to stand in the doorway of his office to find Valeria sitting on the edge of the desk with her elbows resting against her knees while she talked on the phone. She caught sight of him instantly, telling her companion on the other end, "Just a sec, Haven."

Pushing the phone against her chest, she gave him a smile. "Hey, can you put Maria to bed? She wants like a million stories, I guess. I haven't talked to Haven all week, and—"

He shot her a grin. "No worries. I got her."

Val blew him a kiss. "Thanks."

"Make it up to me later."

Her teasing laughter chased him out of the office doorway and continued even when he heard her say, "Yeah, I'm back, Haven."

Heading down the hallway, Chris came to a stop in the doorway of a bedroom that had somehow become a pink disaster zone. And right there in the middle of it was Maria who played with a handful of dolls on her bed. At least, she had managed to tuck herself in.

"Teeth and hair brushed, PJs on, and a drink for bed?" he asked.

Maria looked up from her dolls, grinning. "Done, done and *done*."

He really should thank Bene for teaching Maria that, but ... no.

"Where's Mama?"

"On the phone with Haven. Figured I could read you bedtime stories tonight."

"Okay!"

Chris smiled to himself while Maria rushed to clean her bed free of any toys except for the small pile of books off to the side. Maybe her mother had overexaggerated just a bit. It wasn't a million books. But it was at least ten.

Reading was good for the soul, though.

He didn't mind.

"Tomorrow," Chris said as he navigated the war zone that had become Maria's floor with all her dolls, their accessories, and the sleeping kittens that had somehow found places for their bed, "we're cleaning this room."

"Aw," she groaned. "But why?"

"It's a mess."

"Except I know where everything is!"

As true as that may be …

"We gotta clean it up," Chris muttered, finally making his way to the bed. In no time at all, he'd made a decent place to sit beside a resting Maria with his back against the headboard of her bed. He reached for a book, but she was already handing him one. "*Merci*."

"That one first."

Chris peeked at the cover. "We read it fifteen times this week."

The girl shrugged. "And it's still my favorite."

"What's fifteen more times, then?"

She beamed.

He grinned right back.

Honestly, this was his favorite part of the day. Or really, doing *anything* with Maria always made everything better. He loved his girl. Messy room and all. But they would still be cleaning the damn thing tomorrow one way or another.

Chris made it through three books before Maria handed him the next in her pile. The title? *My New Little Sister*. It made him pause because he hadn't seen the book on her shelves before, and this was the first time she'd ever asked for him to read it. But a quick turn of the page explained exactly where the book came from. The school's library stamp on the title page and the little card on the slot inside said everything.

"Missy has a new baby sister," Maria said, although more to herself than to Chris, he thought. "She said the book was good, so I got it next."

"Oh?"

"Mmhmm. Will I have one, too?"

Okay, *that* made him quiet.

For all of three seconds because kids were smarter than a lot of adults gave them credit for and even when one didn't think they were listening, they probably were. They heard a lot more than anyone thought, and knew more than people assumed.

Especially his kid.

Nearly a month after Valeria's appointment with her doctor where she didn't get her birth control switched, and the two of them had more conversations than he could count about adding to their family. Despite trying to have those chats away from young ears, there was a good chance Maria had heard them talking about it once or twice nonetheless.

Unless she asked, however, he wasn't going to bring it up. Adult conversations were meant to stay between adults unless there was no other choice but to bring it to a child's attention. If Maria didn't outright say she heard her mom and dad talking, then Chris wasn't going to pry the information out of her.

"Would you be happy," he started to ask, "if you had a baby brother or sister?"

Maria shrugged. "Yeah, I think so."

He chuckled. "Only *think*?"

"Well, my room would still be *my* room, right?"

"But you might have to keep it picked up. There's a lot of little things in here that babies don't understand they can't put into their mouth. We wouldn't want that to happen."

"Right," Maria said, nodding once. "I could keep my room clean."

"And share toys."

She sighed. "*Well* ..."

"We can come back to it," he said, attempting to hide his laughter.

"Maybe we should," she agreed, "but I still think I want one."

"We'll see."

• • •

Chris had just closed the door to Maria's bedroom when a throat clearing down the hall had him looking up to find the source of the sound leaning against the wall. There stood Valeria with a frown on her pretty face and an item in her hand that he hadn't expected to see.

A pregnancy test.

"What are you doing?" he asked.

She shrugged as he came closer, and then took the test from her once he was close enough to grab it. It only took a quick look down at the white and pink strip of plastic for him to understand the source of her sadness.

Not Pregnant, the digital screen spelled out clearly.

"My period hasn't started yet," Val said quietly, "but it's been a month, and so I figured I should at least take one and see, right? Maybe we'd be lucky, and—"

"It's only been a month," he was quick to say, dropping the pregnancy test into the pocket of his slacks so that she wouldn't have to keep staring at it. Because clearly she looked at that test and only saw *failure*. Chris was not the same. "Do you know how rare it is to get pregnant the first month of trying, Val?"

"Well—"

"Hey."

In a breath, Chris closed the distance between the two

of them so that he could wrap Valeria in his embrace. There, he hid her away from the world and nothing was wrong. No one could touch her or hurt her. She was too perfect for that nonsense, anyway; too sweet to be sad or anything of the sort.

Pressing a kiss to the top of her head, he murmured, "Just give it some time."

"How long do we give it before—"

"No *befores;* no *buts*. None of that, *mia cara*."

She let out a slow, steady stream of air. "You always know the right things to say, don't you?"

Chris smirked and then leaned in to let her kiss him on the mouth. "Kind of my job. It's what I do."

And he didn't mind a bit.

15.

Valeria

Four months later ...

"MRS. Guzzi," the man drawled from his seat behind his desk, "if you're not one-hundred percent invested in entering a program at this school, then—"

Valeria's gaze narrowed at the bored tone of the admissions officer of the university. "Excuse me?"

"Well, you didn't let me finish."

"Why would I?" Valeria shot back. "You began this conversation with that statement. Assuming I'm not invested in an education, or rather, *getting* one. Is that how you greet every potential student that comes into this office?"

The man said nothing.

Not right away.

Valeria didn't mind.

Ignorant asshole.

It wasn't entirely the admissions officer's fault for Valeria's bad mood, but she figured if he was going to be terrible, then who better to put her mood on? Add in the fact she was four months in to trying for a baby and had yet to get pregnant despite *actively* tracking her cycle—after it returned to normal two months after having the IUD removed—and everything else the doctors and the internet told her she should do, and yet ... no baby.

No pregnancy.

She was starting to think something was wrong. Not that she had anything to give her that indication except for a lack of pregnancy, but she couldn't help the way her mind went. Today, on her way home, she *should* pick up a pregnancy test and take it because she was, once again, two days late for her period.

Same as last month.

Yet, Valeria had a distinct feeling she wasn't pregnant. Once again. Maybe the cramping in her midsection didn't help either, a good signal that her period was going to start *very* soon.

With the stress of *that*, and the attitude of this man greeting her the way he had almost to the second she sat down across from him, and Valeria was just over this day. It wasn't like her to be so short-tempered, but everybody had their days.

This day was clearly hers.

Chris gave her more than enough time—and repeated the sentiment time and time again—to figure out what she wanted to do. He had close to thirty businesses spread across Ontario and Quebec—she could pick one to run if she wanted. Or she could stay home with her daughter. Maybe even go to school.

It was her call.

He said nothing.

Valeria finally decided that she would like to go back to school. Likely for business, or something relating to business. The second she made that decision, she was told to pick a university, and Chris even came home with a stack of pamphlets to help her choose. Any school she wanted, she could go. If they wouldn't *take her* then they would pay her way in.

Val almost wanted to laugh at that—she'd not even finished high school, although the papers Chris brought home one day said she did. A private tutor was ready to be at her beck and call as soon as she started a university to help her along the way.

It was a privilege she'd never had.

Yet, Val wanted to *try* to do this on her own. Take some courses that would look good. Get her GED and work with online courses to add to her list of credits. Would it take longer? Oh, yeah. By a couple of years, but that was the *right* way.

Chris didn't argue.

"You know what," Valeria said, deciding to stand from her chair and leave the meeting altogether, "I don't think today is the right time for this. I have some other things going on, and perhaps I'm just too sensitive right now to discuss something like furthering my education."

Across the desk, the officer folded his arms over his chest and eyed Valeria with a bit more respect than he had earlier. "You're a great candidate for a good many programs at this school, Mrs. Guzzi. The plan laid out in your file to get your transcripts where they need to be is perfect and exactly what you need to do. I hope to see you sitting on the other side of this desk for us to have another conversation when you're ready."

Valeria smiled and nodded. "Me, too. Thank you."

"Have a good day."

"You, too."

• • •

Later that day, Valeria opened the bathroom door to find Chris leaning against the wall where she had left him before entering the bathroom to take her pregnancy test. He took one look at her face and sighed.

"Not pregnant?" he asked.

Valeria shrugged and handed over the test. "No. Again."

"Val—"

"At what point do we move on from it's just taking some time to there might be something wrong, Chris?"

He tapped the test against his hand. A rhythmic *tap-tap-tap* that for whatever reason, she found incredibly soothing. He said nothing and she watched him smack that thin strip of plastic against the palm of his hand for too many minutes to count.

"There's nothing wrong," he murmured.

"That took you at least two minutes to say."

Their gazes met, but he smiled and shrugged even if she was in no mood to be happy.

"Doesn't make it any less true, though," he pointed out.

"But something *might* be wrong," she replied.

"Or we haven't given it enough time. It's like ... there's only a couple days in the month where anything can even happen, Val. We're busy. You run back and forth between here and New York. We have *another* kid who makes us tired a lot of the time. You want to go to school—I have work all over the city all day. Who is to say we're not just ... missing the mark?"

Except she tracked her cycles.

And when they had sex.

She knew ...

Valeria opted not to point any of that out to Chris.

"But," he said quietly, stepping in closer to her with open arms that she took because his embrace *always* made her feel better when nothing else did, "if it would make you feel better, I could see about an appointment with a fertility specialist."

She gave him a look.

He sighed, quickly adding, "*Not* because I think something is wrong, but because I think they could give us some information about what to know, what to look for, and what our options are if it continues like this."

"Yeah?"

"Yeah, babe. I'll do anything you want."

"But you still don't think something is wrong?"

"It's only been a few months, Val. Maybe the universe—or God—is just saying *not yet.*"

Or maybe something was wrong.

Lots of women had one child, and experienced infertility after the fact. There was a whole name for it and everything. She didn't want to worry, but that was kind of impossible. And as each month passed with no positive pregnancy test, she realized just how much she actually wanted a second child.

Chris hugged her tighter like he could read her mind. "Whatever you need, Val. I promise."

16.

"HOW are things here?" Corrado asked. "Heard you've been stepping up a bit more for Papa, huh? Never thought to mention that to me when we talk on the phone. Then again, you don't call as much as you used to."

"Is that what you want? I can check in five times a day if you'd like."

"Don't be fucking cute. I get enough of that from Les."

Chris gave his twin a grin. "If you're asking about business, it's good."

"And you. I'm asking about *you*. Your wife. Little Maria, who by the way, Ginny and her sisters keep asking about because they want to do a sleepover. As though there isn't enough estrogen in my house on a daily basis. All of that good shit, too, yeah."

That had him smiling because all he ever needed to do was think about Val and Maria to make him happy. "It's great, man."

Corrado nodded. "Yeah, I know all about that."

"How's Ginevra?"

"*Very tired.*" Corrado made a noise under his breath. "But so are the rest of us, too. Happens when you have a six-month-old baby in the house, and all that. We're making it work. A bit easier with three people because we can take shifts."

Chris couldn't help but laugh at that. "Shifts, really?"

"Trust me, it works. Coraline is … she still has her days and nights mixed up, or that's what everyone tells me. Really, I just think she likes being up at night, and we're looking at the rest of our lives with that kid."

And yet …

Chris gave his brother a look from the side. "You still

73

love it."

Corrado nodded. "Wouldn't give this up for the world, man. Last week, we were trying to set up the new TV—me and Les—and Coraline just looked at us across the room where she was sitting in her bouncy thing, and she gets quiet before screeching and pointing at us before shouting *Das*. We'd been trying to get her to say that ever since she started saying *Mama* at four months old."

Never had Chris seen his brother light up quite like the way he did right then. Like his whole world was owned and revolved around a blue-eyed baby girl with black curls. And that kid was the luckiest baby in the world because not only did she have one daddy who adored the ground she walked on, but she actually had *two*.

Years ago, he never would have thought his twin would have a kid. Not because Corrado ever said anything one way or another, but because he seemed like he had another path in life to take. Yet, here his brother was with a baby, two spouses, and a whole house full of life and love.

It looked good on Corrado.

He hoped the man knew it, too.

"But anyway," Corrado said, clearing his throat, "she's tired. That's how Ginny is."

"And I imagine she doesn't let you forget it," their father murmured as he stepped into the mansion's office.

"We can never get five minutes away from the rest of them, can we?" Corrado asked Chris.

He laughed. "Well, it is his house."

"He's nosy."

"I am *not*," Gian muttered. "And stop talking about me like I can't hear you. I may be older, but I am not *that* old yet, *figlio*."

Corrado smirked but otherwise, said nothing. That was probably for the better, but honestly, Chris just figured his brother liked ribbing his father once in a while. They all did, but they chose their own special times to do it.

"Ginny wanted me to find you," his father said,

"actually."

"What for?"

Gian laughed. "Coraline won't eat her peas and pears. Oh, and Les just thinks it's *funny.*"

Corrado made a face. "First of all, the peas taste like shit. *I* don't want to put them in my mouth—and I know that because I tried everything she has to eat—so why in the hell would she want to eat them? Second of all—"

"Ginny is right downstairs if you'd like to have this conversation ... you know, with *her.* I just listened to a whole spiel about it from Alessio, son."

His twin gave him a look. "Catch up later, then?"

Chris nodded. "Absolutely. No worries."

Whether or not they would actually be able to catch up was tossed into the air, though. His brother only stayed maybe a day or two, Chris was crazy busy with *la famiglia,* and it never seemed like the right time. He didn't get as much time with his twin as he wanted, but perhaps he should just make some.

Once Corrado was out of the office, Gian turned on Chris with a conspiratorial grin. "And what about you, hmm?"

"What about me?" Chris asked his father.

"Well, I'm told it's not appropriate to ask ... but you are my son, so it's a father's right, no?"

"I have no idea—"

"A baby. Are you going to give me another grandchild?"

Chris choked on a drink of the whiskey in the glass he'd lifted to his lips. Once he had his lungs cleared out, he gave his father a look. "Just come right out with it, don't you?"

"Why not?"

It wasn't that the conversation with his father made him uncomfortable, but that maybe the circumstances weren't entirely right. After all ... it was a touchy subject in his own house let alone someone else's.

"We're trying," Chris settled on saying.

Gian beamed. "*Oui?*"

"It's ... not happening."

Still, his father's smile didn't falter as he crossed the room to come and stand next to his son. "Sometimes, it takes a while."

"That's what I've been saying, too, but we're a few months into it, and ... anyway, we've got an appointment with a specialist in a month. After we come back from the vacation to the Quebec lodge. Just to see or look at options."

"Chris, you're both healthy. Just because it doesn't happen at the snap of your fingers doesn't mean anything. Hell, they won't even look at you for other interventions until you've both been trying for at least a year. Babies usually come when you're not expecting them to, and you're not watching a calendar. *Trust me.*"

He chuckled. "You think?"

Gian patted his shoulder with a supportive touch. "Yeah, I do. Take your wife to Quebec. Enjoy being *with her.* Take her mind off ... well, whatever she's worried about. Go see the specialist if you think it'll help but give it some time."

His father ...

Still the voice of reason, it seemed.

17.

VALERIA *loved* Quebec. More importantly, she loved the vacation lodge the Guzzis owned in the very middle of a massive maple farm. Setting atop a privately owned mountain, in the middle of over two hundred acres of forested land, with a man-made lake behind the three-level lodge for them to enjoy boating, swimming or even fishing, considering they regularly had rainbow trout added every year, it was … perfect.

Nothing like the city.

Not quite like the ranch in Mexico.

Just enough nature and privacy.

Val adored it.

From quadding to dirtbikes, a paintball zone a twenty-minute ride down the mountain, swimming or hiking … they could do whatever they wanted. There was never a reason to be bored when there was always something to do. Including sitting on the small docks leading out to the water to watch the fireflies dancing atop the lake.

She only visited the lodge once before. Shortly after they were married, they came for a weekend to stay with Chris's parents. She wanted to come back almost as soon as they left. So, when he'd suggested it as a week away, even if it meant Maria missing a couple of days of school, Val didn't say no.

Not that they were worried about school for their girl. Maria was smart, her grades were perfect, and the school year was almost over, anyway.

"Are you planning to stay out here all night?"

The voice behind her had Val peering back over her shoulder with a soft smile. Chris stood at the end of the dock, his usual safe distance from the water. Not that he ever actually *said* the lake frightened him, but she knew it had to at least put him on edge. Especially considering his almost drowning happened in a lake much like this one at a vacation home owned by his uncle.

"Thinking about it," she replied.

Chris chuckled. "Want me to come over and sit with you?"

"You don't have to."

"But maybe I want to."

Val winked. "Then, you should do that."

He walked the dock slowly, keeping his gaze on her or the wet wood slapping the soles of his dress shoes. In slacks and a dress shirt that was rolled up to the elbows, his signature look when he didn't throw on a blazer, he looked damn good with the moon high in the sky behind him and the large lodge looming in the distance.

Before long, Chris had come to her side. He took his time removing his shoes and socks before setting them aside. Then, he dropped down beside her on the dock, actually *daring* to put his feet over the side of the dock like hers were. They couldn't quite reach the water, but that was probably okay because it would have been cold.

"I would have come inside," she murmured.

Chris shrugged. "I learned to swim here, actually. *After* the ... incident. This is where Gian brought me. Just me and him. My brothers stayed back in Toronto with Ma. He let me freak out and cry and ... I was a fucking mess, but he put me in the water, and I learned to swim."

"Wow."

"God, I hated him for that."

Val frowned. "I'm sorry."

"Don't be. I needed it. Couldn't even be driven over a fucking bridge without having a panic attack. At least knowing how to swim, it gave me a sense of comfort. And then The League ... well, they didn't fix the fear of the water. They just taught me how to accept the death I'd find if it happened again."

"Jesus Christ, Chris."

His laughter skipped over the lake in front of them. As though his admittance didn't bother him at all, and maybe he just needed to say it to someone else.

Valeria understood that all too well.

"So, we're not going to skinny dip in the lake, then?" she asked, winking.

She wanted him to smile again.

Just for her.

The way he did.

Chris did exactly that. "Probably not, babe."

Then, she had another idea.

"Race you back to the lodge?" she asked.

He hummed under his breath. "What do I win if I catch you?"

"I said a *race*, not a chase."

"I like mine more."

Valeria laughed. "Fine—whatever you want if you catch me."

"*Anything?* Is that a deal?"

A shiver worked its way through her at his suggestion. How was she supposed to refuse? Instead of even trying, she simply nodded, and leaned forward to catch his lips with her own in a kiss as she whispered, "You got yourself a deal."

She stood up and Chris told her, "I'll give you a three second head start."

There was quite a way to run.

Then, he added, "And Maria was down for the count when I checked on her."

Good.

Her kid could sleep through a hurricane.

"Head start is *now*," Chris said.

If he thought his little show would put her off her game, it didn't. Valeria knew from the beginning of this game of chase that she was doomed to lose, if that's what one wanted to call *losing*. But she'd be damned if she wouldn't give Chris a good run for his money even so.

Val's bare feet hit the cold grass, and she heard his loud, taunting *one* and *two* before she chanced the first peek over her shoulder. A laugh pealed out of her when she saw him get up, turn around, and brush his pants off before he came after her.

The man was fit.

All fucking muscle.

She'd come to learn he liked to mountain climb, *and* he did one marathon a year just because he wanted to do something normal. He made it halfway across the back grass of the lodge property before she even made it three quarters of the way to the porch. He caught her before her feet even touched the rear steps with a strong arm wrapped around her waist.

She shrieked.

His laugh came out huskier.

Apparently, *anything* meant her back against the wall of the lodge while he stripped her naked, and then kneeled down looking like sex on a stick to eat her until she was breathing his name into the sky like the prayer that it was.

It was only then that he let her help him out of his clothes. Or rather, just enough so that she was free to stroke his cock between them when he lifted her up against the wall. Hard and hot in her hands, he jerked forward with every stroke. It only took a slight shift of his hips when she fit the head of his cock at her slit, and he was filling her.

Anything meant making her moan.

And scream.

It meant fucking her until her back protested against the smooth logs that made up the lodge's wall, but she couldn't tell him to stop when it all felt so fucking good, too.

His kisses ravaged.

They tasted of *her*.

Suddenly she was reminded that sex was more than just

trying to have a child. It felt like she'd forgotten that over the last while. She loved that Chris was able to drag her back into being a woman with lusts and needs when it was just him and her like this.

She loved her husband.

Entirely.

18.

Chris

"WHY do I always bruise like this whenever I have to get my blood drawn?"

Valeria's question had Chris glancing her way in just enough time to see her pull off the gauze that had been taped to the inside of her elbow. Sure enough, a bluish-brown bruise colored the majority of the spot under the gauze, but he'd seen worse.

"It's normal," he said.

She sighed. "Maybe I just don't like the whole—"

"Everything is going to be fine, Val."

Just like that, she quieted. Her big brown eyes looked to him, and he gave her a small smile that he knew would help to settle her nerves a little more. She was putting on a brave face, considering their current circumstances, but that was just Val. Inside, he had no doubt she was a raging war of anxiety and worry.

"And everything says we just need to give it some time," he reminded her.

"I know, but at least if a *doctor* tells me that, I won't constantly feel like something is wrong with me."

God.

He hated that she felt such a way at all.

Though it was uncomfortable to do in the waiting room's plastic chairs with their *barely there* cushioning and metal arm rests, he leaned over to sling an arm around Val's shoulders. He drew her in close to his side, and she tucked her head against his shoulder. There, he could press a kiss to the top of her head and feel the way she calmed in his hold.

He continued holding his wife like that until their names were finally called by the woman behind the receptionist's desk. Once he'd helped Val to gather their things, they followed the nurse who came to stand at the entry of a hall with a clipboard in her hands. She smiled their way, greeting them by their first names and a cheerful *the doctor will be with you in a few minutes* after she had showed them which room they would wait.

Well, it was more like an office. There wasn't even a *bed*. Then again, Chris assumed a lot of the procedures that happened within a fertility clinic wouldn't take place in regular patient rooms but a better, more sterile environment.

"Sit," Chris murmured, pressing on Val's lower back.

She took one chair, and he took another. The two of them settled into a comfortable silence, and Chris took a moment to look over the different things hanging on the wall. Other than the rows of medical texts sitting on shelves behind the large desk facing their chairs, the walls were mostly filled with pictures of babies and medical licenses.

All good signs, he supposed.

Thankfully, the nurse hadn't lied. Within a few minutes, a knock on the door that hadn't been entirely closed behind the nurse had Chris and Val turning to see a man smiling as he pushed open the door. With lines around his eyes and more white in his hair than gray, the doctor greeted them right away.

"Christopher and Valeria Guzzi, right?" he asked.

"That is us," Chris said.

"Dr. Kennis."

He didn't wait for Chris to stand from his chair before sticking out a hand to shake. He did the same for Valeria who still hadn't said a single word.

"So, you had some blood drawn today, right?" the doctor asked Val as he rounded his desk. "Just to check for some standard stuff, and I was going to have them run a few hormonal checks because oftentimes, that can be the cause of the issues noted in your file. Mind you, you're only a few months into trying for a child, so this wouldn't be concerning for us to begin with."

Valeria let out a sigh. "I did have blood drawn—and good, that's ... mostly what I needed to hear."

The doctor behind the desk chuckled. "Oh?"

"It seems silly, but—"

"I assure you it doesn't. You wouldn't believe how many women *want* and try to get pregnant, and when they don't right away, they immediately default to something being wrong with them. And you know what? When something is wrong, it's more often their partner than themselves."

Chris cleared his throat, but the doctor glanced his way with a smile, shaking his head as he said, "But I don't think there's anything wrong with your husband, either, Mrs. Guzzi."

"Why is that?" Chris asked.

"Well, that blood Valeria had drawn before coming up to the office ... it seems we *did* pick something up. Standard for every blood test is a check of HGC levels."

"Pregnancy hormone," Val said quietly.

The doctor nodded. "Yours is at a level that would suggest you're about three weeks pregnant. Congratulations. I don't think you'll be needing anything from me. At least, not when it comes to getting pregnant right now."

Valeria's wide eyes turned on Chris.

All he could do was smile.

"Val," he murmured.

It was all he could think to say.

"I guess ... you were right," she told him.

Chris laughed. "Probably won't be the last time, either."

"Well played."

• • •

THE FIRSTS

Nine months later ...

Mia Cara made her way into the world on a cold February day. With frost crisp on the ground and a chill in the air, his daughter graced a cold world with her warm life. The hours and hours of her birth had seemed to bleed together to him over the duration, and yet as he sat in a hospital chair in the corner of his wife's recovery room, it was like he could suddenly recall every second of it down to the smallest of details.

Blinking awake in that chair in the hours after his daughter's birth, when the sky was dark outside, and the hospital halls were quiet. After their family had long come, celebrated, and then returned to their homes for the evening.

He remembered it all. Because he would *never* forget.

From the corner of the room, Chris watched his wife coo to their swaddled daughter. Her hospital gown had been pulled aside, showing her naked shoulder gleaming under the dimmed lights. With her dark hair pulled back and high into a messy bun, all the range of love and adoration on her face as she looked at their child was on clear display for him.

He understood that stare.

That instantaneous *love*.

The wonderment of it all.

He'd look at their daughter with the same expression the first time she'd been placed into his arms.

"You're amazing," he told her.

Val looked his way as though she'd known he was awake. "You, too."

Always for her.

BENE & VANNA: PART 3

19.

"THERE?"

"*Mmhmm.*"

"And there?"

"*Everywhere*, Bene."

Bene's chuckles colored the master bedroom of their downtown Toronto penthouse. He kept mentioning that maybe they should start looking at an actual home. With a backyard, somewhere quiet … but so far, Vanna seemed perfectly content with their penthouse in the city. If he were being honest, he was more of a city boy than the suburbs type, too.

But if her wants changed, so would his.

That's kind of how love worked.

He continued working his fingers into all the tight muscles Vanna complained about from the moment she returned home. She *finally* started back to school which meant now she was eighteen weeks pregnant, on her feet most of the day, and too tired to even speak by the time she got home. All he wanted to do was make her *smile*.

Love on her.

Constantly.

Like now.

"Better?" he asked.

Vanna sighed, and rolled over to her back. Those twinkling eyes of hers stared up at him, dark hair spilling over their pillowcases. He couldn't help himself but to touch her—it was an uncontrollable urge that not only drove him crazy, but settled him in a way that nothing else could when he did finally get his hands on her.

"Better," she breathed.

Bene rested down beside her on the bed, reaching out

87

to stroke his fingers through the strands of her hair. Then, those touches of his moved to her neck, too. And just like the sweet kitten she could be when her claws weren't out and ready to kill, Vanna softened and sighed, shifting toward him so that they could tuck in close to one another.

This was better.

It always would be.

"Well," he murmured, wrapping his arms around her and resting his chin on top of her head, "at least you have Christmas break to relax before you have to go back to school."

"*God*, I'll be huge by then."

It took *everything* in him not to roll his eyes. Bene learned his lesson after doing that once to her already because she smacked him for it. When he told his twin, Beni said he probably fucking deserved it because who was stupid enough to dismiss a pregnant woman's feelings about herself? Divert it, deny it, or just love them … but *never* dismiss them.

"It's only a couple of weeks away, and you'll be beautiful," he said. "Same as you are right now."

Tilting her head back on the pillow, she stared up at him. Those soft, pink lips of hers curved into a pretty smile. *That's* what he wanted to see the most.

"Smooth talker," she told him.

Bene winked. "I do what I can, babe. *Now*, what else can I do for you, hmm?"

That smile of hers turned far sexier when he rolled Vanna to her back, and then went with her to hover over top of her with both his hands pressed to the bed on either side of her head. A shift of his lower half had him tight between her widened thighs. The small swell of her midsection—she hadn't really *popped* yet—pressed between them, reminding him all over again, as though he might possibly forget, that this woman was carrying his *baby*.

And goddamn, didn't she look so fucking perfect on her back under him?

He certainly thought so.

Leaning down, Bene kissed her once, and then twice. The third time, Vanna answered his kiss back with her own in a way that had his dick perking to life under his slacks. Her lips parted, and she finally allowed him a taste of her sweet mouth.

Candy.

She always tasted like candy.

"Yes," she breathed against his lips, "you should *definitely* do that, too."

Bene grinned, winking. "Yeah?"

There was *a lot* about pregnancy that he hadn't known or really understood until Vanna was carrying his child. Like *morning* sickness? That shit was a fucking myth. It wasn't exclusive to *just* the morning. And it could be caused by anything from the smell of food cooking to getting up out of bed too fast after a damned nap. Pregnancy was also exhausting, but especially in the first trimester; he swore for those first thirteen or fourteen weeks, his girl slept more than she stayed awake and when she did have to be up, it was to go to school. It wasn't exhausting to *him*, unless you considered that every ad which popped up on his phone was about *baby* stuff because that was tiring.

Nonetheless, pregnancy was a beast.

A whole new monster.

He didn't blame Vanna when she wasn't interested in him because she just wanted to sleep. Or even when she was snappy and whiney because she had the *worst* cravings, yet she knew in a few hours, it was liable to come right back up out of her mouth after she ate it.

Nah, he just … talked to his brothers who'd done this very thing before. And his father. He figured it was all pretty normal, and he just had to wait her out. After all, what was a few weeks without sex compared to the life she was giving him, anyway?

"Love you," she whispered into his next kiss.

"*Ti amo, principessa.*"

Vanna laughed breathlessly when his kisses dotted down her jaw and then made a hot path over her throat. "When did I become a *princess?*"

"The second you became mine."

"Ah, well, I do like that."

Good.

She should.

"One week," he told her, "until we find out the gender."

Vanna fell back to the pillows again, her smile softer than ever. "Are you nervous—I haven't really asked, but do you have a preference for a boy or girl?"

Honestly?

"No," he told her. "I'll be happy either way."

"Yeah?"

"Absolutely, but if it is a boy …"

Vanna arched a brow. "What?"

This conversation had been a while in the making, and he hadn't quite figured out exactly *how* he should tell her about his family's tradition when it came to naming the first boy of a generation. He knew he *had* to tell her, though, because if he didn't … someone else surely would, and he preferred to be the one to do it.

"The first boy of any Guzzi generation is always named Marcus," he said. "My father has it as his middle name—his grandfather was a Marcus, and so was his uncle who passed when he was a younger man. My oldest brother is a Marcus, too."

Vanna blinked. "Oh."

She didn't feel sad. More … *hesitant.*

"It's not modern or—"

She didn't even give him the chance to finish before saying, "Will that even be okay if the baby is a boy?"

Oh.

Now he understood.

Worse, she wouldn't meet his gaze.

Shit.

20.

"YOU know they don't hate you, right? Or us. They certainly don't hate a baby that isn't even born yet, babe."

Vanna gave Bene a look. "That's ... a bit of a stretch when you say they don't hate me. I do, in fact, think some of your family—"

"They don't. We wouldn't be here right now if they did."

His firm—so sure—statement quieted her, but that was fine, too. It allowed her the chance to think about all those gross *feelings* that constantly kept poking up whenever she wasn't ready to deal with them and what she wanted to say next.

Pregnancy was a lot of things ... difficult; *emotional*. Vanna wasn't the kind of girl who cried at the drop of a hat, but yesterday she spilled a glass of milk on the counter and sobbed for a half an hour while Bene sat at the table staring at her like she was crazy. Probably because he didn't have the first clue what to do, and without really trying or meaning to, he often made things worse. *Yep*, she cried over spilled fucking milk.

The irony was not lost on her.

God.

She loved her baby already, though. That was the one clear thing about this entire situation. Though she didn't think *some* people in Bene's family were particularly happy that she was carrying his child, she was behind on school, and she no longer had people from her father's side to act as a family—although, had they ever really been one?—it didn't matter. None of that took away from the ferocity of the love she felt for a child who she had yet to name, and didn't even know their gender. She had no clue if the baby would look more like her, or Bene … right now, she couldn't even imagine actually giving birth, but she knew one thing that was *certain*.

That she loved her child.

She wanted everyone else to love the baby, too.

"Stupid pregnancy hormones," she muttered in a sniffle.

Though she hadn't voiced her inner thoughts out loud, it didn't seem to make a difference to the fact her eyes became wet and a couple of tears dared to escape and tell the truth of the war inside her mind and heart. Still hovering above her in the bed, Bene reached down and wiped the traitorous tears away with the pad of his thumb before they could reach her trembling lips.

"Sorry," she whispered. "I don't mean to cry."

"I've been told that comes with the territory."

She had to laugh at that.

He wasn't wrong.

Besides, Bene was *great*. More than she would ever be able to explain. Even when he thought he wasn't helping her, he truly was. And he *tried*. He made a fucking effort to, for one, make her days better, and for two … he made sure she knew she was loved by him. Every single day he did that, and she loved him for it.

"I'm not sure if something like the traditional name would be welcomed by *some* of the people in your family," she said.

Like his brother, Marcus.

Who currently had the name.

"Actually, it doesn't matter," he told her, "because that's the tradition. So, whether or not Marcus likes it won't make a difference to what the family expects. Because I know that's who you mean even if you're not saying it. *But* … we're not even there yet, Van. We don't know if the baby is a boy or a girl, so I might have just brought this up for nothing."

"But it could be a boy."

Bene smiled. "Could be."

"And if it is …?"

He shrugged. "Then, we'll tell everyone after church on Sunday when we go to my parents' place for dinner."

Oh, God.

"Way to freak me out, Bene," she said, shaking her head.

He leaned down faster than she could blink, his lips hovering over hers with a sinful smirk playing at the edges as he murmured, "How about you let me get back to that *other* thing, and we'll forget all about this one right now, hmm?"

"Oh, the *sex* thing?"

"Yeah, that. Say *yes, please, Bene*."

She pursed her lips. "You're something, aren't you?"

"That's not *yes, please, Bene*."

She loved it more when he acted like this.

So much more.

"Yes, *please*," she breathed, "Bene."

That mouth of his kept going lower with every whisper that left his lips. His *can't wait to fucking taste you*s and his *shorts off now* came out so rough in contrast to the soft ease at which his hands worked against her clothes. He knew her body so well now. Could play it like an instrument he could trace with his eyes closed.

That was why the second he got her silk night shorts off and had nothing separating him from her pussy, Vanna became weightless. She was entirely content to let this man eat her to heaven like only he could. Every hard stroke of his tongue through her slit got her hot and slick before he went straight to her clit until her heart started to hum and all she could do was breathe his name between her fingertips.

It was only once she'd stopped grinding against his mouth, did he hover above her again. He pressed a kiss, wet with her arousal against her shoulder as he slid in behind her. That was how he fucked her. Side by side, her leg lifted and hooked around his thigh, while his hands worked her *crazy*.

His strokes came with an ache. Deep inside, he fucked her with fast, short thrusts that had her falling into a second orgasm faster than she'd ever done before. She had no doubt that before the night was over, the man would have her mind blank and blissed.

They would be *them* again.

Vanna and Bene.

Nothing else had to matter then.

21.

"HEY, did you get that text I—"

"Oh, you mean the meme of the cat?" Bene rolled his eyes, adding, "Yes, Beni, I saw it. You do know I have better things to do than answer your fifty text messages each with a different meme, right? Do you even *work*?"

"First of all—"

"So no, you're not working."

"I'm collecting payments for a Capo, all right," Beni muttered. "It's fucking boring. The least you could do, since you don't want to come visit me in Chicago on a regular goddamn basis, is answer back my texts. Even if they *are* cat memes."

"Does August know about your love of cats?"

"She's allergic."

Bene snickered. "That's ... that's perfect, eh."

"And I don't *love* cats; I like funny memes that make driving on this road bearable—*fucking move, you fucking stupid cocksucker! Who taught you how to drive?*"

He had to pull the phone away from the side of his head because that's how loud his twin's voice was in his ear. It hurt. The one thing a lot of people didn't know about his twin was the fact Beni had terrible road rage, and it only became worse when he was on a freeway where traffic often became backed up.

It was Chicago, after all.

"And now you know the reason I don't visit you in Chicago as much as you want me to," Bene muttered, shifting through the papers on his desk to find the one he needed. Once he did, he could fax it off to the asshole who called about it that morning wanting numbers on a business venture he was attempting with a friend *outside* of mafia business. The asshole being his lawyer because contracts were a real thing, and everything needed to be perfect. "I can't talk for very much longer; I need to head out of here soon."

"What, why? August is busy, Bene. She's got a thing today with Lissa. I need somebody to talk to while I drive."

"That's illegal."

"I have Bluetooth. Everybody has fucking Bluetooth."

Right, right.

"And besides," his twin said, scoffing, "driving while talking is the *least* illegal thing we do in this family, let's be honest."

"Yeah, but people with kids drive on the roads, Beni. Pregnant women. You know?"

That quieted his brother.

"Vanna getting knocked up made you different," he eventually said.

Bene nodded, though his brother couldn't see it. "I know."

"It ain't bad."

"No."

"But it's ... new."

Bene sighed. "Yep."

"What are you doing, anyway? What do you have to run off for?"

"Ultrasound appointment."

"Shit, *yeah.* You're finding out the sex today, right?"

"Supposed to if I can get you off this damn phone."

Because *ah-ha* he'd finally found the paperwork with the numbers his lawyer wanted. Opening the top of the fax machine, he slapped the paper down and pushed the buttons needed to send it off to his lawyer.

"Okay, I gotta—"

"Bene," his brother said sharply enough to make him quiet.

"What?"

"Promise you'll call me right after?"

He grinned at that, and really, kind of wished his twin was there. "Well, we're gonna tell everyone on Sunday, actually," he said. "You're coming into town for dinner, so I thought—"

"*Really*? If this was my first kid, I'd fucking tell you as soon as I knew."

Bene laughed. "Fuck it, I will call you as soon as I know, okay? But I swear to God, Beni, if you tell Ma or Papa what the baby is before I can ... or *anyone else*, I will carve your heart right out of your chest. You got me?"

"You know how I appreciate a good threat."

"Mmhmm. And how I follow through."

"Right, got it. Hey, what if there's *two* babies in there?"

"Beni, there's one. One single baby. We've heard the heartbeat."

"Yeah, but I heard about some twins that hide behind the other, and you can't see them until they're on—"

"The ultrasound, yeah. But we had one of those when she was like ten weeks just to check on size and everything. We saw the baby. There's only one, and that's it. Back to my threat because I was fucking serious."

Beni grumbled under his breath. "Fine. No telling. My phone will be beside me."

"Better be."

He barely got the call with his brother hung up before the phone beeped with yet another person trying to reach him. He had a damn good mind to ignore it altogether, but when he realized who it was trying to get a hold of him, he knew that he had to pick up the phone or he would be in a hell of a lot more shit with his father. Considering the thin line he was already walking inside their *famiglia* and with business, well, he tried not to push the rules set out for him any more than he had to. Things weren't great with other men in their mafia, but he made it work. At the moment, it was the best he could do.

It was all his father and brothers asked for.

"Kevin," Bene said, picking up the phone, "what can I do for you today?"

"I've got a problem with the asshole on the east side."

Bene's brow dipped. "You mean the Capo—"

"Yeah, that asshole. He's pushing his lines with me again. We've had about fifteen sit-downs between Chris and Marcus about it. I called Chris this time and was told to call you. Apparently, you made friends with the fucker and he likes you, so you can go see him today about this problem."

Why?

Why was this his life?

Oh, he loved it.

He wanted to be a made man, and now he *was*. He wasn't a Capo yet, probably wouldn't be for a while. And he did a fuck lot more running for other people than he wanted to. Really, he probably hadn't deserved his button and a few people liked to make it known they thought the same, but otherwise ... business was good.

Except on a day like today.

"I'm kind of busy—I can run over in a few hours, though," Bene said.

"Nope. Now."

"But—"

"Call Chris, if you don't fucking like it. You're now the go-between. That's what I was told."

Fuck.

Bene knew better than to call Chris, Marcus, or even his father and ask for special treatment. It didn't matter what today was or how he promised to be there with Vanna when they found out the sex of the baby. The mafia was what it was—it had to come first, even when he sometimes wished he could put it last. Sure, his brothers would probably work it out, and so would his father, but he didn't want *them* to feel like they had to treat him differently than anyone else, either. After all, hadn't he done that enough before?

"I'll be there," he told the Capo. "Just fucking relax, man."

"*Right*. Later, Bene."

Yeah, he'd show up to chat with the other Capo. Right after he made a phone call to someone else, that was.

22.

Vanna

GOD.

Why did she have to use such big purses?

Every time she needed to find something in her bag, Vanna never could because the item she searched for would be the *one* lucky thing to fall to the very bottom under all her makeup, wallet, snacks, a half a dozen receipts, and … why did she have *so many pens*?

"Like, where did you even go in there?" she asked no one in particular.

Except the stupid phone that had somehow managed to get lost in her purse while she stood outside on the sidewalk in front of the clinic where in just ten minutes, she needed to be inside to find out the sex of her unborn baby. She wanted to call Bene back just to make sure he was absolutely positive he wasn't going to make it in time, but also to find out who in the hell he was sending in his place since he said that's what he was going to do.

She figured … his ma, maybe.

Or even Valeria, if she wasn't busy.

Oh, and did she mention that she had to pee?

Because she did.

Badly.

Apparently, a woman needed to have a *painfully* full bladder to have an ultrasound done at nineteen weeks so then the tech could get a clear picture of the baby. Seriously, if she coughed or sneezed the wrong way, she was going to lose her bladder all over the sidewalk in her cute maternity dress and kitten heels.

Wouldn't that just top this day right—

"You okay?"

At the familiar voice—one she had certainly *not*

expected to hear—Vanna finally took her attention away from the purse with the black hole somewhere inside it to stare at the man now stepping up on the sidewalk a few feet away from her. In his usual suit, he offered a smile that felt hesitant, but still seemed true.

Didn't make her less confused.

Or nervous.

"Marcus," Vanna said.

Marcus cleared his throat and glanced toward the clinic. "I was closest when Bene put out a couple of calls about getting someone here to be with you for your appointment because you'd probably need a ride home after. I might have mentioned you would possibly not like that—mostly *me*—but he said you would be fine. So, here I am."

Straight to the point.

As always.

Vanna nodded. "Um, well thank you. For coming, I mean."

Could this get anymore awkward?

Probably.

She wasn't going to test the theory out, though.

"Well, let's go in," she said. "My appointment is in ten minutes, and I guess they want me to pee in a cup … apparently I am supposed to be able to magically stop my urine flow on a full bladder because I can only pee a little."

Marcus made a face. "What?"

"Nothing … pregnancy shit."

"Oh. I'll stay out here and wait, if you want. I don't have to go inside and sit in the waiting room."

Things were not … great with Marcus. Clearly. They still had a way to go, but he made an effort. The same way Bene and Vanna did for him. She had to give him credit for that, and she appreciated the respect he offered her even when he didn't have to do that at all. She understood perfectly fine that the man felt as though Bene and Vanna had betrayed the family … or rather, she did and then Bene protected her after the fact. If there was anything someone should know about Marcus above everything else, it was how close he held his family and how much he loved and protected them.

To him, she had been a threat.

At the moment, she thought he was trying to decide if that was still the case.

"Would you come in, though?" she asked. "Inside the room with me to see the baby? Bene was supposed to be here, and … I mean, if something is wrong, I'd like to have somebody in there."

Marcus tipped his head to the side. "Do they think something is wrong with the baby?"

"No, but—" But *what if?* Statistics on the internet that could be found with nothing more than a simple search would drive a first-time pregnant mother *insane*.

Quickly, the man across from her seemed to understand what Vanna didn't *want* to say. "Hey, I get it. Sure, I'll come in."

Vanna smiled.

So did he.

This time, it didn't feel hesitant at all.

"Thanks, Marcus."

"Don't mention it."

• • •

"Everything looks great," the ultrasound tech said, moving to grab the bottle with the cold blue gel once more, "so let me put a little bit more of this on, and we can check to see what this baby is hiding between his or her legs. You did want to find out the sex, right?"

Vanna nodded. "We did, yeah."

"And Daddy is—"

"Ah, that would be my younger brother, not me," Marcus said with a chuckle when the tech turned on him. "I am here for … moral support."

Yeah, why not?

That worked.

"That's nice, too," the tech said.

"So, the baby was good?"

"Perfect size. Measuring just right. The heart looks strong, and everything else is just as it should be …." The woman trailed off after she squirted a bit more of the blue gel on Vanna's stomach, and put the wand right on top of it to smoosh it around on her slightly rounded stomach. "Okay, let's see what we can find."

Vanna's gaze stayed glued to the screen as once again, her baby took shape in shades of gray, white, and black. In the background of the white noise, they could hear the beating heart loud and clear. Something else to calm her nerves. Then, the wand moved quite a bit lower on her belly, and she couldn't quite make out what she was seeing on the screen as the tech hummed under her breath and inched a bit closer in her seat.

"Oh, there it is," the woman murmured. "*Very* clear picture, huh?"

Vanna blinked. "Is it?"

A laugh came from the tech.

"Well, I suppose I look at them every day, so I know when I see one or the other. Congratulations, Vanna, you're having a boy."

A sharp inhale came from the corner of the room. She turned to see Marcus tip his head back a bit as he watched the images on the screen with a soft smile and kind eyes.

"The first Guzzi boy of his gen," Marcus murmured, passing Vanna a look as he shrugged under the weight of his navy blazer. "He's destined to be amazing, and we haven't even met him yet. That absolutely does deserve congratulations, Vanna."

Quietly, all she could think to say was, "Thank you."

23.

Bene

TEN *minutes.*

That's all Bene had left before he'd arrive at the penthouse. He could make it in eight minutes if he was willing to push the speed limit any more than he already was, but he figured … better not to take the chance, all things considered.

He'd not called or texted Vanna. She hadn't done either for him. Maybe a part of him just didn't want to ruin the surprise before he got home, or it could have been that he wanted *her* to tell him straight from her lips what the sex of the baby was seeing as how he couldn't be there to hear it first with her.

Not to mention, after an entire day of dealing with a spoiled Capo who had been allowed to continue his nonsense for longer than anyone else would be afforded, he was ready to be *home*. With his girl … always with her. She made everything else worth it.

Tomorrow, he could call his father and tell Gian someone had to actually deal with the Capo on the east side this time because warnings, threats, and what little punishment he had gotten before now for his behavior was not deterring the fool from causing issues with a neighboring Guzzi man. They couldn't have that pettiness because it always led to something bad.

But not today.

He'd deal with it tomorrow.

They had time.

Six minutes, he thought as he blew through a yellow light that was liable to turn red at any fucking second. The nice little camera on the lights would have caught his license plate, and he'd get a ticket in the mail, but since he made it before it turned … *winning.*

Bene had just turned onto his block when a call started ringing throughout the speakers of his red Lambo. Cursing under his breath and not even giving the automated system a chance to tell him who was calling, he muttered, "Answer."

A second after the speakers crackled, a familiar voice filled the car. "Bene—hey."

"Marcus."

"I just got home. Thought I should call and—"

First things first, he had some shit to say to Marcus.

"Thank you for going to the clinic today, but if you know what the baby's sex is and you tell me before she can, I swear to *God*, man, I will drive all the way to your place just to beat the hell out of you."

Silence echoed.

Then, Marcus chuckled.

"Fair enough," his oldest brother said.

"But yeah," Bene said, clearing his throat, "thanks for going there. I know you probably didn't want to, and you had a million other better things to do than entertain us today, but it means a lot."

It took Marcus a second to respond. The silence felt weighed down by a lot of things they had yet to say to each other. Frankly, Bene didn't know if they were ever going to really sit down and discuss everything that had happened leading up to this moment. Maybe they didn't need to, and each side simply had to process their feelings about it alone.

Either way …

"It's not a problem," Marcus eventually replied.

"Yeah, well …"

He'd just pulled into the underground garage for his building, already snatching up all the items he had sitting on the passenger seat, so he didn't have to waste anymore time than he already had before he could get home.

Stepping out of the Lambo, he slammed the doors shut

and moved for the bank of elevators toward the far end of the garage. The Bluetooth in the vehicle switched to the one in his ear as he pulled out the fob that would open the elevator with a press of a button once he was close enough. Sometimes, it paid to be rich. Especially in a city like this one.

"I gotta go," Bene said, "because I just got home."

"Right, but hey."

"What?"

Marcus made a noise; one Bene couldn't decipher. "Just … water under the bridge, all right? If you or Vanna need something—*anything*—you call me, okay?"

All at once, Bene's trek to the bank of elevators came to a complete stop. He swore the noise in the underground garage silenced as he took in his brother's words and tone. For a second, he just stood there staring at the cement wall to his right.

"Bene?" Marcus asked.

He dragged in a lungful of city air. "It's a boy, isn't it?"

"You didn't want—"

"It's a boy."

He didn't even pose it as a question that time. What did it matter when he already knew?

"Yeah," Marcus said, "it's a boy, Bene. Congrats, man."

This time, it was Bene who went quiet.

"You still there?"

"Yeah, uh, I was just thinking. What if it had been a girl, Marcus? Would it still be *water under the bridge*, or …?"

"Yes," Marcus said instantly.

"Why?"

"It's about family, Bene. The baby—boy or girl—is family. Maybe I hadn't really settled myself on the fact there was a baby until he was on that screen today. And I just … shit, my bitterness isn't worth family not being *family*. So yeah."

"Yeah," Bene echoed.

What else needed said?

24.

Vanna

THE hot bath water soaked into Vanna's skin and calmed her senses. Vanilla clung to the air, compliments of the bubble bath she'd poured into the tub while it filled. She also dimmed the lights in the room and lit the floating candles that floated in the large Jacuzzi tub.

It wasn't that the day had been *hard*. Quite the opposite, really. She just needed a moment to decompress and process everything. Not just the fact she was pregnant, but also that now she knew what she was having—a little boy.

Sometimes, people needed a second.

Vanna was one of those people.

She'd managed to zone into the sound of her favorite singer belting a ballad from the speakers of her phone resting on the counter that she hadn't even heard the bathroom door creak open. It was the shadow of his form crossing over her in the water that had Vanna lifting her gaze to find exactly who she expected. She wasn't scared— couldn't be when it was *him*. No matter what, if the two of them were in the same room, she swore she could find him just from the feeling of his presence alone.

God.

She kind of loved that.

"Babe," Bene murmured.

She found his dark eyes looking her over in the tub, and then falling on her nineteen-week swell that barely peeked out above the hot, bubbly water. Subconsciously, maybe, or perhaps it was just a need to touch her little bump, she pulled her hand from the water to place it overtop her stomach. Beneath her palm, the baby shifted.

"I wonder if he can feel the warmth?" she mused. "He moved."

It wasn't *big* movements. Some pregnant women—not that she knew a lot of them, but she talked to women who had been pregnant before and also stalked online forums because she needed *someone* to talk to sometimes about this—said it could be uncomfortable. Vanna had yet to get to that point in her pregnancy. Right now, her little guy's movements were all flutters and pops inside her belly or against the surface when she pressed her palm to him.

"Do you think so?" she asked Bene again.

Overhead, Bene smiled. "Probably."

She couldn't help but grin at the way his smile turned soft the longer he stared at her. "What is *that* for?" she asked, pointing one dripping wet finger at his face.

"Hmm?"

"That … *that* smile, Bene."

"You, mostly."

Vanna laughed, and dared to cut her hand through the top of the water and bubbles so that just a bit would come out of the tub to splash him. "*Mostly.*"

He barely reacted to the new wet stains on his slacks and dress shirt. She didn't know where he'd thrown his blazer after arriving home, but that was fine, too. There was something to be said for the way Bene looked in dress shirts and dark slacks. The way the fabric molded to all the hard, fit lines of his body was art, really.

It should be appreciated.

Vanna tried to admire it as often as she could. Thankfully, Bene just happened to be vain enough that he enjoyed her perusal. Not that she was any different in that regard.

"Also," he murmured, kneeling to rest one of his arms along the tub and be at eye-level with her, "because you said *he* when you mentioned the baby. Didn't even realize, I don't think. But I heard it."

Ah.

Yeah.

Vanna nibbled on her lower lip. "So, *yeah*, the baby is

a—"

"Boy," he finished for her, leaning in before she could even take a breath. His lips found hers in a kiss that had her burning up for entirely different reasons than *just* the hot water she currently rested within, and she didn't mind a bit. There was something *sinful*, but also loving, about the way he kissed her in that moment.

Vanna didn't want it to end.

Although, when he did finally pull away, it was only to dot the sweetest of kisses over her face. Down her jawline, over her cheekbones, and across her smiling lips. She never had to wonder if this man *truly* loved her. He showed her that he did in more than enough ways. She adored him more for it, too.

His hand found her cheek while his thumb stroked back and forth. Vanna sighed into the touch, turning her face against his palm to press a kiss there. She watched him through the thick veil of her lashes, waiting for him to say something first. It was easier when he talked; everything about this life, she found, was easier with *him*.

"I kind of figured it out before now," he admitted.

"Are you happy?"

"Vanna, I was always happy. I am *still* happy."

She dragged in a quick breath. "Yeah, you were. You're right."

Bene grinned. "But now that I know, it's time to start filling that kid's closet. *All the brands*. A whole rack full of shoes. Yes, I have *many* plans. I also have to call my twin. I promised I would."

A laugh skipped from her lips.

"Call him, then," she told him, "and don't go *crazy* buying things. Everybody else will, too. We'll have *too* much and that's just a waste."

"Not in this family."

She knew better than to argue. The Guzzis were what they were—*disgustingly* wealthy just happened to be one of those things, and they did not apologize for it.

"But first," he said, standing up and unbuckling the belt at his waist, "we celebrate, even if that means soaking for an hour in the tub with you."

"I thought you were calling—"

"I will. *After.*"

"Oh, so we're *just* soaking," she prodded when he shoved his pants down.

He gave her a wink. "We'll see."

Right.

She knew what they were going to do just fine. The anticipation was already curling through her like a tight coil about to break. She couldn't fucking *wait.* The desire for sex had come back full force now that she was smack dab in the middle of the second trimester of this pregnancy, and that was just fine with her.

"Oh," Bene said, making quick work of undoing the buttons on his shirt, "and on Sunday, expect *someone* to mention we need to figure out something for a wedding, and soon."

"You think?"

"Oh, yeah. Probably my father."

"I'll keep it in mind."

Bene passed her a look. "Do you still want to?"

"Get married?"

"Yeah, babe."

Vanna didn't even have to think about it.

Of course she did.

"Why wouldn't I want to marry *you*?"

His dark laughter echoed in the bathroom. It heated her up all over again. So did the last kiss he leaned over the tub to tease her with before deciding to finish undressing. Once he'd finally wrestled out of all of his clothes and fell into the tub with her, the water crashed over the edge of the tub. Bubbles floated with it. Even one or two of her candles that were meant to just float in the water.

She laughed at his mess.

Loved him anyway.

But that laugh of hers was quickly drowned out when he fitted in behind her and pulled her into him. She found a hold on the edge of the tub with each hand. His one hand dove up her back to tangle in her hair while he stroked his cock hard using the crack of her ass to grind against him.

She also loved that he sometimes just wanted to *fuck*. A lot like her. No muss, no fuss—just *sex* because shit was so good. He could play later. Make her sing in bed when he ate the taste of himself mixed with her right out of her cunt.

For her, he had no shame. Not in his want, or what made him hot, or how he wanted to mark her in ways that only he would ever know or see.

He treated her like a deity.

He worshipped *oh*, so well.

How had she gotten so lucky?

25.

Bene

"ARE you nervous?"

From her seat on the passenger side of the Lambo, Vanna flashed Bene with a brilliant smile that had him grinning right back. "No."

"Not even a little bit?"

She shrugged. "Nope."

Good.

That's what he wanted.

"But," Vanna drawled, pointedly giving the two-seater Lambo a look, "you might be nervous when you realize you'll soon have to replace this car with something more appropriate."

"Like *what*?"

"Something with a back seat, perhaps. Even better if that back seat can fit a baby's car seat."

Bene scowled. "How did this conversation get turned around on *me*?"

Vanna's laughter followed their car right through the gate leading to his parents' mansion. Bene *really* hated to admit it, but she also had a point when it came to the car he loved. Before, he might have said he loved the car more than most anything in the world, but now he knew that wasn't the case.

As he eased up the winding driveway, he said to her, "I'm not getting rid of the Lambo—it's my work car."

"*Work*. That's hilarious. You let the engine on this thing roar if you're just going a block to the damn store, Bene. I'm pretty sure you got two noise violations for that last month, too. It's more than just work for you when it comes to this car. Come on."

He grinned.

She wasn't wrong.

"*Still*," he said when she gave him a look from the side, "it's got just enough work done in it to get me from one side of this city to the other in half the time. You know, as long as there's no fucking traffic in the way."

"And there always is."

Bene sighed. "Yeah, basically."

Soon, they had parked in the large circular drive heading his parents' mansion. The car stopped purring when he put it in park and cut the engine. He made a big show out of giving the interior a longing look before his gaze settled on a smirking Vanna in the passenger seat.

"You really think I'm getting rid of this car, huh?" he asked.

"Not really."

"Good because I'm not."

"I knew it," she scoffed.

"But there *is* a new four-door Mercedes SUV on the lot right now with *your* name on it. We just need to go over there and sign for it. I was thinking … after dinner with my parents?"

"It's Sunday—"

"They'll open the lot to sell that car, Van."

She pressed her lips together, *trying* to hold back her smile. And failing beautifully, too. Before she could say another thing, he leaned over and caught those sweet lips of hers with his own in a long, slow kiss. It was just what he needed before they would head inside and spread the news about their baby boy.

She didn't have to be nervous. He'd be edgy enough for both of them.

• • •

"Look at you—your bump is so tiny … *cute*," Cara praised.

"Not jealous *at all*," Valeria added in the chair next to

his mother.

Vanna laughed, giving Valeria a look even as she took Cara's hug. "Don't worry, I'll be as pregnant as you soon enough."

"Yes," Val agreed, "but I only have a few weeks left, and you—"

"I only get bigger from here, don't I?"

"Basically."

"But it's worth it," Cara added quickly, winking.

Bene knew better than to laugh, but the exchange *was* a little comical. Instead, he rubbed the back of his hand against his mouth to keep the laugh at bay and any proof of his amusement thoroughly hidden. With more than one woman in their family pregnant at the same time, not to mention *emotional* ... well, better to leave that right alone.

Yeah.

Nobody ever said he was dumb.

"So, who all knows what this baby is?" Cara asked, giving Bene a look by peering around a still-standing Vanna.

"No one, Ma."

"Lies."

Vanna snorted under her breath. "No getting shit past her, huh?"

Cara smiled. "No, there is not."

"Marcus and Beni," Bene admitted. "That's it."

"Two entire people that aren't me? *Two, Bene*?"

"Awe, Ma—"

"*Two!* Gian ... *Gian!*" she shouted for his father who quickly came into the dining room for the adjoining kitchen with a raised brow and dark eyes narrowed because his wife was yelling. That never spelled good things for the person making her yell. "Did you hear what *your* son just said to me?"

Gian's stare turned on Bene instantly. "No, I did not."

"Listen, Marcus kind of had to know, he went *with* Vanna to her appointment. No one else was in the city. I literally called everyone," Bene rushed to explain. "And I had to tell Beni, the asshole made me promise and *everything*, Ma."

"I did," Beni called from somewhere in the kitchen. "I'm his twin, technically it's like the kid is half—"

"No, it is *not*," Bene called back. "He is entirely *mine*, thank you. You want a fucking kid, then go have your own."

Silence coated the dining room. It took Bene entirely too long to realize what he had done in those few seconds prior. The way his mother's smile turned soft, and his father's stance eased up from the other side of the room made him drag in a heavy breath. However, it was Vanna's amused grin that she shot over her shoulder that really did it for him.

He said *he*.

"It's a boy?" his mom asked.

Bene shrugged. "Yeah, Ma. The baby's a boy."

"You have *zero* tact," Vanna told him.

Yeah, well …

"Surprise," he said, even throwing his hands out for good measure.

The laughter that came from every room had Bene sighing again and shaking his head. But hey, so was his life … and damn, he *loved* this life.

"Now," his mother said, "*when* are we …" She pointed between the two of them, adding, "And by we, I mean you and her, getting *married?*"

"Yes," his father murmured from the kitchen entryway, "I have also been waiting for that announcement. You know what we agreed, Bene."

Right.

It had to be before the baby was born.

At the moment, Bene was less worried about that and more concerned with handling the pretty red that covered Vanna's cheeks. No one else but him seemed to notice, and he was quick to cross the few steps keeping them separated so that he could get her in his arms.

Or rather, he wrapped one arm around her waist while his free hand dug into the inner pocket of his suit blazer to find a little box he'd been keeping hidden all week. The ring finally came in—he was never going to *not* ask, and he wasn't going to just give her any ring from a jewelry store; it had to be perfect. As perfect as she was for him. He wouldn't just marry Vanna because he was told to, and she deserved a proposal, and her own big day and whatever else she wanted, too. He planned on making sure she got all of those things and far more.

Starting now.

Pulling the white velvet box, he forgot about the other people in the room. Between them, he popped open the top to showcase the large oval diamond sitting on a band of white gold that reflected every light on each cut of the gem.

"The answer to *when* I plan on marrying her," Bene said, giving Vanna a little smile, "is whenever she tells me yes."

Vanna's hand on his arm tightened as she whispered, "*Yes.*"

26.

Five months later …

"KNOCK, knock," came a smooth voice.

Glancing up from her swaddled newborn, Vanna found Marcus standing in the entry of her private hospital room. Though she was tired and sore and *amazed* at everything that had happened over the last forty-eight hours since her arrival at this hospital, she still managed to give her new brother-in-law a smile.

"Hey," he said.

"Hey, Marcus."

"Sorry. I didn't mean to miss it. I just landed an hour ago and came right—"

"It's okay; you mostly missed Bene freaking out when they took me in for a c-section, and then the L & D ward threatening to call security if the family didn't quiet down after he was born and Bene went out to announce it."

Marcus laughed under his breath, still staying right where he was and not coming an inch further. "Still, I didn't mean to be out of town when everything went down."

"Life never goes as planned."

She'd learned that well enough.

"Could I …?"

Marcus's question trailed off, but the way his gaze dropped to the baby she was currently rocking in the corner chair told her everything he hadn't finished asking.

"Of course, he just ate, and now he's sleeping. Bene ran down the block to get me a burger and fries. Hospital food *sucks*."

Truly.

117

"I don't want to wake him up, or anything," Marcus said.

"You won't. Come here."

She would have gotten up and taken the baby to him, but right now, moving wasn't such a great thing. It wasn't so bad to rock the baby but to get up and *walk*? *Ha*. No. Absolutely not. It felt like her midsection was ripping apart at the new seam it now sported.

Marcus took his steps slowly and careful, not making a single sound as he came to stand in front of Vanna. "I guess nothing went as planned while you were here, huh?"

She sighed. "Not really, but it's okay."

Really, it was.

All she had to do was look at her baby boy, and she knew that above all else. Everything that happened didn't matter when she stared into his little face. He looked *so much* like his father, but also took a little bit of her, too. He had her hair, though, but dark, hazy eyes that everyone had assured would clear up soon enough and let her see their beautiful color. He didn't cry as long as someone was holding him, and if it was *Bene* who rocked him, the boy would fall asleep in three minutes flat. It was cute because the baby would keep his eyes peeled all the way open to stare up at his father until all at once, he'd close them and fall asleep.

She wanted an unmedicated, natural labor, preferably in one of those birthing tubs with her new husband close by, dimmed lighting, and a playlist of her choosing echoing in a *very* quiet room. God, they had planned the best they could for that even taking birthing class after class just so that she could do what she wanted when it all finally started.

Instead, the baby wouldn't budge.

Neither did her cervix.

Then, when little man's heart rate dropped dangerously, the doctor made the call. She remembered very little about being prepped and taken in for the surgery. She did, however, vividly recall the first cry of her newborn when they pulled him from her body.

And how Bene *cried*.

Yeah, that was kind of perfect. Did the rest have to matter? Not when she had a healthy baby.

"God, he's perfect, huh?" Marcus murmured.

Reaching down, he pulled the swaddle away from the baby's chin to get a better look at his face. Marcus chuckled under his breath, and traced a single finger over the baby's features.

"Looks like every other Guzzi boy," he noted.

"That's what literally everyone has told me."

"I bet that was nostalgic for Ma."

Vanna nodded. "Yeah, she didn't want to let him go."

"Did you pick a name?"

"We did. Marcus Gian Guzzi."

Her baby wasn't the first of his name, but she bet he would do the most amazing things with it. And wasn't that what counted?

"Decided on the same, then?"

She smiled. "It seemed to fit."

"Hey, man. Glad to see you finally made it back."

Vanna handed over her baby to Marcus while Bene quietly closed the door behind him. He patted his brother's shoulder on the way by, and gave his son a quick kiss on the top of his head before bringing the bag of greasy takeout straight to his wife. Once she had the bag in her hands, she tipped her head up for a kiss. Bene gave her exactly what she wanted, but then pressed another softer kiss to her forehead.

"You good?" he asked, murmuring the question.

"Yeah, so good."

"Did you ask him yet?"

"Ask me what?" Marcus asked.

The two of them leaned sideways to get a good view at Marcus holding his nephew. Rarely did anyone see the man being soft and kind, but whenever he had a baby in his arms, he turned into a giant teddy bear. Even now, it was like no one existed but Marcus and the baby he held.

It was sweet, really.

"We were thinking," Bene started, grinning, "that maybe you would like to be our son's godfather. I mean, you're the first of your gen, and he's the first of his. He might need somebody who understands what that means, Marcus."

Finally, the man looked away from the baby. "I thought—well, what about Beni?"

"I talked to Beni," Bene replied. "He gets it."

Marcus stared down at the baby. "Can't really say no to that, could I?"

Bene chuckled. "Not really, no."

"I wouldn't, anyway."

Yeah.

They had known that, too. It was just how this family worked.

No matter what, they were still family.

BENI & AUGUST: PART 4

27.

BY far, one of the best things about August Guzzi's job for Manic Media was that they gave her free reign to do what she thought was best. When it came to her spreads in the magazine, and the articles that she poured hours of her life and love into, those reading it could trust it was one hundred percent *her* in those pages. There was nobody looking over her shoulder judging possible projects because her boss trusted her to know—better than anyone else—what *her* audience wanted to see.

At twenty-seven, August had *finally* reached a level of success where, when she handed over a completed project with her team, there were no questions from higher ups, no changes to make her articles easier to digest to certain groups of people, and that was that. It hadn't always been easy, and there were the occasional bumps in the road when she took the job at Manic Media, but all in all … she regretted nothing. She wouldn't change anything.

Which was why, when a week ago, an artist from Los Angeles contacted someone on August's team with a story about an up and coming rapper who stole their artwork for a recent album release, and even plastered it across merch, no one questioned her decision to chase the story. She didn't even ask if she could chase the story, but rather, let her boss know what she planned to do.

Everything was a go.

Just like that.

Yes, she was told, *get the artist's go-ahead, do the interview, and then let us know where you want to go from there.*

No questions asked.

Hayden Frankson, a digital artist *just* breaking onto the scene in LA, shifted in the chair across the table from

August. Dragging his fingers through the dreds he kept tied back in a bandanna, he shook his head. "He's going to *bury* me in legal—"

"Not necessarily," August interjected fast.

Better to get the man off any topic that could possibly lead him to a decision where he backed out of this interview with her. Right now, that's *all* it was. Just an interview to go over the story he had to tell, the proof he was able to provide about the rapper and the art he stole, and then possibly where they could go from there. Be it through legal action, something with Manic Media, or maybe even both if the guy liked the idea.

However, they would go nowhere—and she wouldn't be able to help the man at all—if he decided the threat of backlash from media, the public, or otherwise might just be too much for him at the end of the day. Not that she couldn't sympathize with his feelings in that regard. God knew she had been *canceled* in one way or another online because a group of trolls decided she had too big of a mouth with opinions they didn't like.

Once was because someone decided to dox her even though nothing about her life was very private when she had been online—and so was her work—for *years*. If someone looked hard enough, they could find whatever they wanted about August.

Not that she encouraged it.

Yeah, her situation wasn't exactly the same as Hayden's, but the end result might be if they didn't play their cards right.

The artist sitting across from her dragged in a quick, shaky breath. Around them, the coffee shop with chrome and green accents kept the hustle and bustle going but other than the large latte in front of her, she really wasn't there to enjoy the scenery or atmosphere. She didn't need the man to tell her how nervous he was even just *sitting* there. It was obvious in every dart of his gaze whenever the chime over the door rang to say someone new had come into the shop.

"Do you want to do this on another day?" August asked. "If so, I understand why, and we could catch up another—"

"I contacted a lawyer yesterday."

"Did you?"

Hayden shrugged. "Yeah, I figured … better to know what I was looking at on the legal side of shit, you know?"

"And?"

"He told me to defend my copyright. That it would make a precedent for other artists and in the industry in general. Said a bunch of other shit, too, but that's all legal jargon I really didn't understand. You know what a buddy of mine said about it all?"

August set the pad and pen in front of her on the table, ready to just listen for a while instead of asking questions that she might be able to fit into an article. Sometimes, she had to put the journalist side of her away and bring out herself. A human, with a heart and feelings, because people needed that more than they needed the views, clicks, and engagement she could bring to the table.

"What did your friend say?" she asked.

Hayden let out a hard laugh, the frustration bleeding through when he muttered, "That I should be *grateful*. Exposure, and all. A fucking joke, really. Like Tay-J putting my art on his shit—without even asking if he could—is gonna pay the bills. *How*? The guy didn't even credit me. That's not the kind of exposure I want, anyway."

"Is this? Because you should consider that, too. If you don't want the exposure of problems from his side of things, be ready for the backlash this *will* cause. Either way, it'll happen. It's just a matter of what you control while it happens."

That made the man pause.

"What options do I have from here?" he asked quietly. "Because from where I sit, it all looks like one big uphill climb."

That was the real question, right? At least, he knew what he was looking at. It was a step in the right direction. Better to know than to be hit from the side with it.

"Going a legal route is a good start," August said, "and so was contacting me. Because I can get you and your work into the public eye before Tay-J's team even has a chance to respond in any meaningful way. If we can spin the court of public opinion in your favor rather quickly, then I can almost guarantee it'll be settled faster than you could blink. Likely without much spotlight because they'll have enough to deal with as it is. It's just a matter of setting you in the right position to do these things. You understand?"

"Not really," Hayden muttered. "I just wanted to make some art."

August smiled, knowing that feeling all too well. "Thing is, you're still making art. This isn't going to stop that, regardless."

"You think I should defend my copyright?"

"Absolutely."

"And you're willing to help with … publicity and—"

"I wouldn't have flown from Chicago to here if I wasn't willing to leave Los Angeles with something tangible to hand back to my editor," August replied. "Something that will help you, for the record. I'm not in the business of selling my morals for clicks."

Hayden nodded. "Okay."

"Really, *okay*?"

"Yeah, okay. Let's do this."

That was all August needed to hear. Grabbing the pad and pen, her gaze scanned the questions she had already prepped for this meeting. Already, she could see the article-style interview forming in her mind, and how she wanted to open it.

What happens to art when the artists are forgotten?

It felt like a good headline. One that could catch attention. She could already see the bold, black, block font taking shape across the page, leading the reader into the opening paragraph where in just a few words, she would already have them ready to devour the rest of the article. At the end of the day, the writing was still August's passion.

What she did *best*.

Because the truth that followed would certainly make everyone think; when artists were forgotten, they stopped making art.

"All right," August said, feeling the buzz of her phone down below in the bag at her feet. "Let's circle back around to when you found out they had stolen your art for the album. We'll go from there. Sound good?"

"Sure," Hayden replied.

As he drudged up the details of an event she knew had to be traumatic for an artist that was still relatively unknown in his industry, she reached down to pull her bag into her lap. Digging through it to find her buzzing phone, August was entirely unsurprised to see she had three missed calls.

All from her husband.

Beni's contact, with the three black hearts she'd put beside his name, lit up the banner on the home screen. The last notification wasn't even a call, but a text.

Love you, babe, catch up later, okay? I know you're busy, he'd written.

She was always busy. So was he, lately.

No doubt, he wouldn't pick up if she called back. A quick glance at the time told her that he was probably on the south end of Chicago like usual. Doing … whatever he did.

She learned not to ask. Things worked better that way, but this was their life.

God knew she loved it.

And *him*.

She loved him.

That's what mattered the most.

28.

Beni

THE one regret Beni Guzzi had as he pulled up to the private airstrip on a mid-January evening? That he'd told his wife to go ahead to Los Angeles without him. Not that LA was his thing or that he had anything to do there while she handled work of her own, but hell ... he bet it was a lot warmer there than it was when he stepped out of his black BMW Roadster.

The car—a gift to himself for his recent twenty-sixth birthday—would be parked in a nearby jet hangar owned by his uncle, the Outfit's boss. Until he returned from the business trip, anyway.

He'd miss the car.

Barely even had time to drive it so far.

God knew winter wasn't the best time to have it on the road, and he would pay for it come spring when it would need a touch-up anywhere that the salt on the road dared to touch the paint ... but hey, it was still worth it.

Mostly.

"What are you doing taking that car out in this weather?"

Beni chuckled at the question, turning away from the driver's door to see the familiar figure approaching through the falling flakes of snow. "Can't help but take it out, can I? *Look at it.*"

Tommaso did, his cousin humming an appreciative sound the closer he came to the Roadster. With all its sleek lines, the blue accents he had done on the top and mirrors of the car certainly added to the sexy appeal. Beni still loved his superbike but even he wasn't crazy enough to bring that out in the winter.

"Certainly draws attention," Tommaso replied. "And

you know how *everybody* feels about that, Beni."

"Not you, too."

Tommaso gave him a look. "What about *me*?"

"Listen, I get enough shit between my father, *your* father, and every other made man who thinks I'm too flashy for their liking. You can't give me all this money and expect me not to do anything with it because people will stare. That's all I'm saying."

And he was sticking to that, too.

Fuck what the rest thought.

"Well," his cousin drawled, eying the car again.

"Yeah?"

"That's fair. The car is ... a bit much, though. I mean, *for* winter. Let's be fair, Beni. Nobody is foolish enough to take a vehicle like that out on the roads this time of year. You're asking for trouble, and I don't mean just from the mob. How do the tires even *stick*?"

He had a point.

Not that Beni would say so.

"You just worry about what you're driving. How about that?"

Tommaso rolled his eyes and turned with a wave of gloved fingers. "Whatever, come on, you're already late. Theo's waiting."

"I'm not *already late*. I'm five minutes early."

"Except he's already on the jet, and you're ... out here running your mouth, man."

Well ...

Fine.

"Are you coming this trip, or just seeing us off?" Beni asked.

"Just here to see you off. You know how Dad is with me and the guns."

Right.

The boss of the Outfit preferred to have his son under his feet more often than not. Beni understood the reasons why, of course. If men were looking at Tommaso as the next man to take over the family, then … he should *be* placed where he could be watched at all times. Better to be seen and known in this business than forgotten.

Beni wasn't quite the same.

A couple of years back, he took up working under Theo's portion of the Chicago mob. While the man handled his position as the front boss—with Cory Rossi as well—he also had a major hand in the Outfit's gun trafficking business. Something Beni found he was pretty good at when someone offered him the chance to get his hands into the pot as well.

It was better than running for Capos.

Or the streets.

Beni pulled his phone from his jacket, checking the screen to see if his wife had replied to his latest message about leaving town last minute. A lot of his work with Theo was done like that—a call came through with a time and a place for him to be, and that was that. He could question it if he wanted, but it almost always promised he wouldn't get a call for the next job or meeting … or *whatever*.

His wife had replied.

It made him smile.

See you when you get back. I love you, Beni, she had written.

No questions.

No problems.

That was usually how it worked between them now when it came to their life. He wasn't the only one constantly busy with work or *something* that wasn't about them. This was what they had signed up for together, though. She put her career first and so did he even if their jobs were worlds apart. If anything, his constant hustle taught him to respect hers as much as he did his own.

So, he tried not to complain.

Mostly.

Sometimes, it was hard.

Especially when all he wanted was his wife. Preferably at

home in their bed. Spending quiet mornings together where nothing mattered but them. It didn't matter as long as the two were together.

Life wasn't always so kind.

"Put the phone away," Tommaso said when they stepped up to the side entrance door to the private hangar. "Shut it down for the trip. We don't need any towers watching where we are, right?"

The paranoia, man.

It never ended.

"Let me tell my wife goodbye," Beni muttered.

As though he hadn't already done that.

Really, he just wanted to reply in kind to August's *I love you*. He did, all the while Tommaso stood there with the door open like he didn't have time for any of it. Once he was done, Beni shut the phone down and gave his cousin a look.

"Happy?" he asked.

Tommaso lifted one shoulder. "That's a matter of opinion, and I find it's better if I don't have very many of those. People tend to share more of their own with me, then, and I learn interesting things that way."

Just like his father.

Not that Tommaso realized it.

"Here's an opinion for you," Beni muttered, stepping past the man to enter the hangar where he found a jet waiting in the middle of the large space. "I haven't seen my wife in almost a week, and it'll be another two before I do. So, less bitching from you right now might improve my mood ... but who knows?"

"Mmm, Cam said Aug headed to Los Angeles for something, right?"

"*Work*, not something. She has a job, man."

"I know that." Tommaso sighed behind Beni and clapped a hand on his shoulder. "I'll tell you the same thing my father tells me whenever I complain about how much running I do for the Outfit."

"Which is what?"

"Learn to make time, Beni. Nobody is going to give it to you in this business. That's not how it works."

Right.

Make time.

Giving the waiting jet a look while considering the fact it would be another two weeks before he would be back home ... when the fuck was he supposed to make time?

How?

Tommaso gave him a look from the side, and as if he could read Beni's mind, said, "You'll figure it out. We all did."

29.

THE last half hour of August's day when she was in the office always found her enjoying the time she had alone. Or usually. She tended to spend those thirty minutes going over any appointments she had the next day or reorganizing *something* ... she could never leave anything alone or the same for very long before she wanted a change.

Her desk wasn't an exception to the rule.

That was why her assistant found August surrounded by a mess of her own making, mostly comprised of the different things she had yanked from her desk and put on the floor to *envision* her new workspace.

Danielle didn't even blink a lash at the sight. The girl was used to it, now. "Well, I was going to ask if you were busy, but ..."

Picking up the glass bowl she used for mints and hard candies, August straightened to her full height with a laugh. "Not any busier than I usually am this time of day. What's up?"

"Uh, just a last-minute meeting. I forgot to mention it and—"

"With whom?"

Because that was all August cared about.

Danielle only grinned. "He'll be here in two minutes."

That didn't answer her question. August set the glass bowl to the edge of her desk where it would be more easily accessible to anyone on the other side—and less to *her*, since she really needed to lay off the sugar—and turned to tell her assistant exactly that.

The girl was already gone, though.

Poof.

Like she hadn't been in August's office in the first damn place. *What is going on?*

That wasn't like Danielle at all. She had only been working as August's assistant for a few months—her last girl ended up going back to college when she figured out media wasn't the best place for her focus during her internship at Manic Media.

She kind of missed her.

She *did* like Danielle, too.

Usually.

Reaching for the spot on her white desk where the phone had typically rested, August had every intention of calling Danielle to ask her to come back in the office but stopped with a shake of her head. The phone was still on the floor waiting for a new spot on her desk. And she had unplugged it to keep the wires from becoming yet another mess for her to handle.

Just another day in the office.

Nothing new to see.

"Something wrong, babe?"

At the new—and entirely *unexpected*—voice, August spun on her heels to find a man leaning in the doorway of her office. A man that shouldn't be there. Not that she didn't like the sight of Beni grinning her way because she did. More than he would ever know. In his leather jacket and dark wash jeans, he screamed the fun time she knew he could be, and nothing was better than that.

He also wasn't even supposed to be in the country.

"What are you doing here?" she asked.

Beni lifted one shoulder, winking as he stepped into her office, slamming the door behind him. He didn't even glance over his shoulder as he did it. "Making time, August, that's all."

"Time for what?"

"Us."

He said it like it should be obvious.

Maybe it was.

She was still a little stuck on staring at him, drinking all of him in because it was the first time she had laid eyes on him in two weeks. Sure, they chatted at night when he called from a number she didn't recognize. Those ten-minute phone calls weren't nearly enough to satisfy the need she had for her husband, though. Not that she ever told him that.

August didn't want to make Beni feel like there had to be a choice between *them* and his work. After all, he never did that to her.

"So just to fill you in," Beni said as he grabbed the handle on the shades for her office window, twisting them to shut out the view from the outside. "I only have a couple of hours in Chicago. Nobody is even supposed to know we're here before we head out again. I managed to get away while I had the chance ... and here I am."

His gaze was back on her.

Hot.

Determined.

Wanting.

August recognized the lust reflecting in her husband's stare. She didn't need to be told what he was feeling or needing when he moved toward her. She could sense it in every one of his steps, in the way he reached for her when he was close enough, and how it soaked from his aura to hers the moment he had her in his arms.

His lips locked over hers, those hands of his sure and knowing as they skimmed over her braids and down her back. The flick of his tongue against the seam of her mouth had her parting her lips for him before he could even ask for it.

Then again, maybe that was him asking.

She had more questions.

When would his business trip be over? How long would they get together before one of them had to run off again for something else? Was life ever going to slow down?

But his kiss silenced her.

It ripped away those thoughts and instead, replaced them with a hunger that was never too far from her mind whenever she was close to this man. The same way the ache started up between her thighs couldn't be abated even when he lifted her to the desk.

"Open up," he growled against her lips.

August grinned but did as he said, widening her thighs for him to step in between. Before she could even blink, he had her skirt yanked higher, wrinkling the silk fabric. And without a single care, too.

Not that she minded.

Beni was already working apart his belt.

His impatience had her laughing.

"You came here today just to get laid, didn't you?" she asked.

He grabbed her chin, tipping her head back so that she was forced to stare up into his eyes. Leaning in, he placed one sweet kiss to her lips, and then another. "You fucking know it, babe. Been missing you—and *this*—for weeks. Now shut up and let me fuck you while I have the chance."

She didn't blame him.

Not one bit.

The second his hands were between her thighs, pulling her panties down her legs, August knew this was the best way to end her workday. It certainly wasn't how she expected it to end, but that was just fine too.

Once he had her panties discarded to somewhere—the floor, the desk, did it matter?—he was back between her legs. He kissed her while his fingers worked her into a wet, breathless mess. It took so very little for him to work her up and get her crazy.

Beni knew her body. Like an instrument made just for him.

He had her singing his name in mere minutes, catching every single one of her breathy moans with his kiss to muffle the sound while his thumb toyed with her clit, and his fingers filled her full. A stroke, then a twist of his digits, another circle of his thumb and ... *God*, she was going to fall apart.

Right there on her desk. Spread open for him. Definitely not her usual workday.

"There ... *right there*," August gasped, her orgasm coming on fast as Beni smirked knowingly against her mouth. "Don't you dare stop—"

"Wouldn't *ever*," he murmured. "Give it to me. Come for me. I *want* it."

She did.

Entirely lost to him.

She barely felt the loss of his hand between her thighs before he was fitting himself at her hot, wet slit. His grasp was back on her chin, but now a little lower. He held her head back to watch him while he took her. One inch at a time until she was full of him, trembling, and trying to hold onto the edge of her desk for *any* support.

She found none.

He fucked her like that, too. Fucked her crazy and wild. In her office with the door closed, hiding all her sounds so that no one knew what was happening just beyond the shut blinds. He always had to make things *fun* ... even sex.

It was kind of perfect.

She truly did love this man.

30.

Beni

"BENI?"

The call of his name followed the *click* of a closing door. He didn't answer his wife's call, still hoping he might be able to surprise her even if she always seemed to know whenever he was near.

"I gotta let you go. August's back," he told his twin.

On the phone call, Bene laughed. "Yeah, better let you go, then. Wouldn't want to hear what's about to come next, huh?"

"Fuck you, man."

Bene's laughter still rang in Beni's ear long after he hung up the call and discarded the phone to the bedside table. He still called his brother once a day—or more if he had time. Otherwise, if he didn't make time to call his twin, then Bene sure as hell did. The asshole could blow up a phone like any clingy female. Not that he dared tell his brother that.

But his trips to Toronto had become more and more sporadic over the years as business picked up, and the mafia took higher priority in his life. He truly understood all those warnings from his father. Gian tried to make them all recognize *and* respect the sacrifices of made men.

Yes, they had wealth.

Privilege.

They were feared.

Adored, too.

But they also sacrificed more than anyone knew to be these men. Not that anyone cared to hear their complaints because at the end of the day, did it matter when they were only *criminals*?

Yeah, Beni finally got it.

He'd tell his dad that but then Gian would get into one of his *I told you so* attitudes and nobody needed that. Especially not him. Besides, he figured this was one of those lessons that really didn't need more discussion after it was learned. It just … *was*.

"Beni, are you home?" his wife asked the quiet house, her footsteps echoing up the stairwell.

He resisted the urge to answer August back if only because now she was closer to finding him anyway. Not that he intended to hide but when he got back from the business trip, he headed straight to their bedroom to empty his bag. But the bed looked *really* fucking good, he dared to sit on it, and the next thing he knew, he was on his back, arms behind his head, and staring up at the ceiling.

Ready for a nap.

Almost.

There was something about *his* bed. The bed he shared with his wife.

And their home. They bought the place in Melrose a little over a year earlier. Sure, they were fine living in the penthouse apartment, but he couldn't deny there was something appealing about the whole *house* thing. A house with a yard, a little fence all the way around the property, and the way August lit up when he suggested they start looking at properties.

Anyway.

Whatever it was, it called his name until he was there and happy. What else needed to be said?

"You couldn't answer me or what?" came the sweet voice from the bedroom doorway.

Lifting his head up just enough that he had August in his line of vision, Beni offered her one of his signature smirks and replied, "Thought you might like a treasure hunt, that's all."

Her dark eyes glittered when she lifted one eyebrow in response. "Oh? And what *treasure* is that?"

He could have said a lot of things.

Better things.

Instead, what came out of his smartass mouth was, "The treasure in my pants, babe. Obviously. Let's be real, we know why you married me."

He was still foolish.

He had too much fun.

At least, he had a wife that didn't mind and let him be as stupid as he wanted to be. August's laughter was the only warning he got before she chucked her purse in his direction. Beni barely managed to catch the leather bag to keep it from hitting him square in the face. Tossing the bag aside, he found his wife was already coming his way.

Opening his arms, he caught her when she fell on top of him in the bed. Instantly, they were a tangle of limbs and hot kisses that made him forget how tired he had been only an hour before when he first crawled into the bed. Not that he was mad about it.

Or about to complain.

August rained her sweet kisses over his lips and jaw, her fresh manicure dragged teasing lines against the pulse in his throat where his heartbeat gave away the truth of exactly what she was doing to him. Not that he could hide the length of his erection, either, once he had them rolled over on the bed. Fitted tight between her wide thighs, he ground against her center, his tongue darting beyond her parted lips for another taste while her soft groan filled the bedroom.

"Missed you," he told her, pulling away just far enough to stare at her.

Sometimes, he wanted that.

Just to *look* at this woman.

She was perfect.

Entirely his.

What more could he want?

August's brown eyes watched him under her lowered lashes. "I think you know *very* well that I missed you, too."

"Could still tell me."

"Like I need to feed your ego anymore than it already is Mr. *Treasure In My Pants.*"

Beni couldn't help but laugh.

And *damn*, it felt good.

"But was it a lie?" he asked, grinning.

She just shook her head. "You're terrible, and I am *not* encouraging that nonsense. Trust me, I have learned my lesson. And for the record, your dick was only *part* of the reason I married you."

Well, wait a second …

"What was the other reason?"

August winked and as fast as he had rolled them over to be on top, she changed their positions. But then she climbed off of him, too!

"Where are you going?" he demanded, half-embarrassed at how high his voice turned when he was staring at her back disappearing into the attached bathroom. She just left him there with a raging hard-on like he could take care of it himself and *hell no*. "August!"

"I gotta pee!"

"Oh."

He shut up, then.

While his wife did her business in the bathroom, he heard her ask, "How did the trip go?"

"Good. Theo made the deal. Not that I expected anything else. We're just waiting on a call to confirm some dates, and we'll be making a run."

"Huh. Good. Right?"

"Yep, it's great, babe."

That was the extent of the conversation, and August didn't press for more even as she came out of the bathroom while drying her hands on one of their white towels. She never asked for more details than what he gave when it came to his work and the mafia, although sometimes he knew she wanted to. He appreciated that she didn't all the same.

"So," August drawled, her tantalizing grin coming back as she tossed the towel to the bedside table and leaned over Beni's form on the bed. "When are you heading back out?"

"Anytime."

She made a face. "Really?"

"Anytime this month."

"Are you still coming to New York with me to see my parents?"

"I'm gonna try," he returned.

It was the best he could do.

"As long as you keep trying, that's what matters to me," she whispered.

Then, she was back in bed. *With him*. Wrapped in his arms. Taking every single one of his kisses. Letting him strip her bare, so he could climb between the heaven that was her thighs and love her the way he did best. The way that had them both seeing *God*.

Shit wasn't always great.

It was, however, still perfect.

Like August had said ... that's what mattered.

31.

AUGUST *tried* to keep her irritation in check as she packed her carry-on bag that she would take on the flight with her to New York, but it was easier said than done. *So to speak.* And it became obvious that she wasn't hiding it well between her current phone call, and the man leaning in the bedroom door with his apology written all over his face.

"Babe, I'm sorr—"

August held up one hand, quieting Beni while she finished up the call with her editor. "So, everything is definitely a go for Hayden's story?"

"Absolutely. Are you okay? You're very ... short."

That was a nice way of saying her tone had been a little too snappy for the entire conversation. It wasn't like Trisha was at fault or the cause for August's current mood, but she also didn't share more details about her private life than she had to. She thanked a rather large social media presence—and the constant trolls—that liked to glom onto any detail they could to spin it in their hateful ways. She tried not to feed the trolls. Even if that meant she kept a distance and a barrier between her work and her private life.

Then, when she did the same thing online, no one expected anything different. It wasn't like she needed to see photos of her husband and his family splashed across her social feeds again with attached headlines like *Viral Reporter Paid by the Mob.*

It wasn't good for her.

Or Beni.

Well, it wasn't good for anybody.

Honestly.

"I'm fine," August said, tampering her tone as much as she could even though the anger in her heart was still very present and flaring with every word she spoke. "I'm just running a little late here to catch my flight. I'll get a hold of Hayden and let him know we're set to run the article next week—email me everything to send over to him as well, please?"

"Absolutely," her editor replied. "I will get my assistant right on that. You'll have it in the next ten minutes. How does that sound?"

"Perfect. Thanks."

"Have a good trip, August. You deserve the break."

Right.

Except the trip wasn't going as planned, and it hadn't even started yet. That didn't make the rest of it look very great. Not that she told the woman on the other end of the call any of those details.

"Thanks again," August replied. "Bye."

She didn't bother waiting for Trisha to reply in kind before she hung up the call. Tossing the phone aside to the bedspread, she continued packing the carry-on bag because she really *was* running late and if possible, she didn't want to have to run straight from security to her gate at the airport. She enjoyed finding a place to sit, grabbing a drink, and maybe listening to a few minutes of an audiobook just to relax.

Flying wasn't her favorite thing.

Especially when it was commercial.

"Aug—"

"Beni," she said sharply, giving her husband a look from the side that screamed for him to *shut up*. The smart man he was, he did exactly that in the doorway, even going as far as putting his palms up in surrender. "You promised you were going on this trip with me."

"I said I would *try*. And I did. I can't help that they just called me an hour ago. If I could head to New York with you for even a day, then I would. Theo isn't letting me do that. It's not like I can tell the asshole *no* or something."

"Can't you?"

Her question was pointed.

Heated.

A warning if she ever heard one.

Beni didn't miss it when he sighed heavily and replied, "You know it doesn't work that way. I can't just tell people no, August. And what's *really* going on, babe? This isn't like you. You don't get pissed when plans change. It's not like this is the first time we've had to change shit last minute. I'm sorry. I am."

She knew he was.

And he was right, too.

This wasn't like her at all. In fact, leading up to the New York trip, he had repeated on more than one occasion that it was possible he might have to pull out for work. Despite that, she still hadn't expected it to happen when they were just hours from getting on the plane.

"I only wanted to have a week," she muttered, reaching for the hardcover paperback that she would read on the plane if the audiobook was trash. It was always good to have a backup, right? "You know, without work, and … your mom is even coming to spend a couple of days, Beni. *With us*, but now it'll just be with me, and I'll have to explain why. You know I hate doing that even if Cara never says anything one way or another."

Not bothering to say more because she figured her disappointment was clear enough, and there really wasn't much her husband could do at this point, August finished her packing. Just as she zipped the bag, a ding from her laptop sent her across the bedroom to check the email that had just come in. Likely from Trisha's assistant with all the details and a finalized spread to send to Hayden in Los Angeles. His legal recourse would begin the day *after* the article went live. Everything was looking good for that.

If only the rest of August's life would follow the same path.

She couldn't be so lucky.

What was with her emotions? The damn things ping-ponged back and forth faster than she knew how to handle them. Dragging in a breath that she hoped calmed her nerves, August clicked into her email while Beni crossed the room to stand behind her. She said nothing as his arms wrapped around her from behind and his warm, soft mouth found the back of her neck.

He gave her a soft kiss.

Then, another.

She loosened up in his hold.

"I am sorry," he murmured against the shell of her ear.

"I know."

"How about we figure something else out when I get back ... and you're back, too, I mean." Each of his words accompanied another hot kiss to a spot on her neck. While she loved it, entirely too much, they also didn't have the time for what Beni was trying to start. She was too lost in what he was saying to care or tell him to stop, though. "We could do a trip to Toronto, make it a weekend thing. Shit, Bene's been talking about wanting to go to the Maldives this winter, too. We could do that? I promise *nobody* will step in the way. Okay?"

Well ...

August clicked out of the email, half aware of the time that was ticking by with every second she wasn't on the road to the airport. Only half, though, because Beni was still kissing the back of her neck, *and* her email had her attention again.

Or rather, the newest email.

A notification, it seemed. Sent from one of the apps on her phone that she used to track her cycles. It would also let her know if something was up or didn't look right. The app also sent email reminders when she forgot to log her period. Which was what it had done.

Except ...

August blinked at the screen, seeing the dates and

understanding what it possibly meant.

"I gotta run," Beni said behind her, obviously not reading over her shoulder. If he did, he would realize the app email said she was five days late. "I need to catch up with Theo and Tommaso."

August was *never* late.

Ever.

Her mind ran the gamut of reasons how this might have happened and why she missed it. Of course, it all boiled down to the same thing—she *was* late, and the rest was unimportant if that meant she was pregnant.

"Love you," he told her.

She clicked out of the email, murmuring, "I love you, too."

But also thinking, *that might explain the crazy.*

Just a little.

Was she pregnant?

32.

Beni

ONE of the better things about getting his button—his *in*—to the Chicago Outfit was that Beni no longer did the grunt work. He wasn't so prideful that he couldn't admit he was a bit of a spoiled bastard. Something that more than one person had pointed out to him over the years.

The privilege and wealth that he grew up surrounded by was not actually afforded to him when it came to the mafia. There were no servants to do his work. No one to answer to his many bosses when he didn't want to be the one to do it. No, it was just him.

And his spoiled ass.

Just because he was a born millionaire with Guzzi as his last name didn't mean he wasn't expected to get his hands as dirty as everyone else when it came to a Capo's crew. Especially when he was supposed to be *part* of the crew. Everyone was treated equally, for the most part, unless they were someone's favorite.

That had not been afforded to Beni.

His uncle might have been the boss of the Outfit, but at the end of the day, he was the same stupid fuck as anybody else trying to get his button. The only difference that his raising and last name allowed him more than others was trust. He *knew* this life. They knew that he knew it. There was no question about his loyalty to their life, the cause, or the family. Shit, he took a bullet to the chest trying to protect this thing of theirs.

He was here until he was dead.

That was that.

Which was why, he knew, his button had come rather easily compared to so many others who still weren't any closer to getting theirs than they had been years ago. Men vouched for him when the time came because they trusted him.

Where he came from.

Who he was.

His last name.

And yet, despite no longer having to do the grunt work when it came to a job, Beni still found a certain respect and dignity when he got down and dirty with the rest of the crew. Which was why he found himself waist-deep in packing peanuts surrounded by ten other guys in a rundown warehouse as they packed boxes.

Boxes of guns, that was.

For the run.

"You look like you're having a grand fucking time," came a voice from Beni's left.

Sticking his middle finger high, Beni replied to his cousin, "Eat shit, Tommaso."

"Not my style. What are you doing?"

"*Helping.* Give it a try. Makes this go faster."

Tommaso made a noise under his breath before saying, "I think not, yeah."

Right.

Well, Beni didn't blame or fault Tommaso for his desire to let everyone else handle the dirty work of packing the guns and getting them ready for transport. Like him, his cousin had been born into more privilege than he knew what to do with when it came to the mafia. And at the same time, Tommaso had also been given very little of that privilege when it came time for him to earn his button. If after everything, as a made man, he didn't want to fuck with the bullshit and just be the man who made the calls ...

Who was Beni to tell him not to?

Different strokes for different folks.

He liked that motto.

"Let's go, let's go! *Faster, boys!* I want this shit done before the sun sets!" Theo's shouts bounced off the warehouse's walls, echoing back to Beni's spot. He gave Tommaso a shrug, but then laughed when Theo came into view, pointing at Tommaso. "And *you* … you fucking help, too. Stop standing around like a *cafone*."

Tommaso gaped. "But—"

"*Work*! Nobody's kissing your ass tonight, Tom."

That was that.

In the next second, Tommaso had grabbed a box and a bag of packing peanuts. His grumbled complaints flew over Theo's head when the man spun on his heel and headed for the same office he had just come out of to yell at the rest of the crew.

"That's some shit," Beni told his cousin, laughing. The sight of Tommaso in his designer suit with pink packing peanuts stuck to him as he dumped a bag into a box was one he wouldn't soon forget. That was for sure. "Now fucking look at you."

This time, Tommaso gave him the finger.

Beni only shrugged.

It was good, too, though. Working like this with his cousin, the rush of the gun run coming up with time ticking down … all of it, Beni lived for it. He was sure Tommaso felt the same in a lot of ways even if the asshole whined a bit while it all happened.

So was their life.

They asked for this.

"This is the last run for a while," Tommaso said.

That perked Beni up. "Yeah?"

Tommaso shrugged, moving one box out for another. "Yeah, Theo wants to lay low for a bit after this one. Let any heat die down, you know? Anyway, we're looking at a few months or more before he's even going to entertain another deal, and then it'll be a while before we've got to run the guns, right? A break is good."

Really fucking good.

"Think I might slow down, too," Beni said. "After all this, I don't know."

Resting his arms over the boxes, Tommaso grinned. "Why? Ready to *really* settle down, Beni? What, are you thinking two-point-five kids to go with that picket fence you painted white for August last summer? Never took you for the type but I mean, your twin did it … I guess it's only expected that you were next, right?"

"Fuck you."

The two laughed.

But yeah.

Beni shrugged, adding to his cousin, "Probably exactly what's gonna happen. I mean, what else was I going to do?"

Right?

33.

"SHE is definitely your wild child," August said to her sister-in-law, Ginevra.

She laughed in response, not the slightest bit offended at August's observation of her oldest child, Coraline.

"I blame the boys," Ginevra replied, an easy shrug falling from her shoulders as she grinned at the sight of her four-year-old daughter *running* across the monkey bars. *On top*. Like the kid had no fear of slipping and falling. Down below, her two-year-old brother, Lev, stared up at his sister in total wonderment. As though he planned on being the next one up there doing the exact same thing. As soon as he figured out how. "Corrado and Les let them ... do whatever."

On August's right, the other woman who had joined them for their day out laughed lightly. Cara, her mother-in-law, had the idea of the park earlier when the kids wouldn't settle long enough for them to eat a late breakfast at a restaurant nearby.

They just need to run off some energy, she had said.

She wasn't wrong.

It was also incredibly endearing how much Cara Guzzi loved her family. Not just her sons, no. Their wives. The grandchildren they gave her, too. All of them. In fact, her mother-in-law made it one of her first priorities to make sure each of her five sons' wives knew how much she adored and appreciated all of them in her own ways. Usually by spending individual time with the women in a way that was specific to something they enjoyed.

For August, Cara never missed a thing that was published with her name attached. She was always one of the first people to congratulate August and was forever

151

wanting to chat about her articles and accomplishments beyond the surface. Because she cared and she wanted her daughter-in-law to know it. They also shared a love of fiction, and regularly kept up on what the other was reading and what they thought of the book.

If anything, it showed August that Cara was more than just her mother-in-law. She was also someone she counted as a friend. One of her very best.

"The word *no* doesn't exist, hmm?" Cara asked, still smiling over at Ginevra.

"Not in our house, apparently."

Cara only shook her head, still seemingly amused, while she fixed the cashmere shawl around her shoulders. Turning her attention back to the playing children, she said, "It's not a bad thing to let children find their own boundaries. There are, however, many times when setting boundaries can lead to bad things. Do we let them find and know safety through exploration or overprotect to their possible detriment? Something to think about."

"True. Which is what Alessio likes to say, and Corrado agrees, of course. Sometimes, it scares me to death," Ginevra replied, nodding at her daughter who was currently making a second trip across the top of the monkey bars. "Like *now* ... Coraline, you be careful up there!" Then, under her breath, she added, "Gonna give me a fucking heart attack, kid."

"Okay, Mama!"

The sweet, unbothered reply of the four-year-old carried over the park. Little Lev was still observing his sister like she was his hero for the day. It made August think that what Cara said about kids finding their own boundaries through exploration made sense—to an extent—especially if the boy watching his big sister had just learned there was nothing to be scared of when it came to the monkey bars.

Considering he'd cried when she first climbed on them, clearly wanting her to come back down where he thought it was safe. Or, that's what August assumed.

Who knew what was in the mind of children?

Or *babies*.

Speaking of which ...

August suddenly found it a lot harder to sit still on the bench between Cara and Ginevra while the pregnancy test she had taken—several, actually—sat in her purse on the ground. Three tests, to be exact. One for each day that she had been in New York visiting with her family and Beni's, too.

"How's your mom and dad?" Cara asked at her side.

She swallowed the lump forming in her throat to say, "Good. They want to do dinner tomorrow and since you're in town ... Ma said the table is open for you to join if you want."

Cara lit up, beaming. "Of course. It's been too long since I saw them. And since they're one of the only in-laws I have ... I try to make time, you know?"

She did know very well.

Sometimes, August wondered how Cara found any time for herself when she spent so much of it with everyone else. Then again, maybe that was where the woman found most of her happiness and peace. The family was something the Guzzis held in the highest of regards. No excuse, the effort would be made for blood. And even those who had been welcomed into their family through marriage, like August's parents.

"So, when are you and Beni going to get on this train, anyway?" Ginevra asked, the question coming out of the blue without warning.

"What train?"

Ginevra grinned, showing off white teeth. "Kids. *Babies*."

Oh, God.

There it is ...

The panic must have been written clearly on August's face because her sister-in-law was quick to reach over and grab her knee overtop the denim skinny jeans she had pulled on that morning. Might as well wear them while she still could, right? Well, there were *some* cute maternity clothes that she could probably pull off.

"I was just kidding!" Ginevra said, her remorse tugging away at her smile. "I'm sorry. I know you guys are really focused on work, and you have so much going on. I didn't mean—"

"I think I'm pregnant," August blurted out.

There.

She said it.

It wasn't the first time, though. She told her mom while sitting in the airport where she had grabbed her *first* pregnancy test. It wasn't that she wanted to keep it a secret, but it was one of those things ... how exactly should she bring it up?

August didn't know.

So, she just *said it.*

The responding silence from both women sitting on the bench on either side of her had August drawing in a long breath before she said, "So yeah, that's a real thing right now."

"You *think?*" Cara asked quietly, her tone kind and warm.

As it always was.

"I keep saying think," August returned.

"But?"

That time, it was Ginevra encouraging her to keep going.

August's cheeks pinked as nervous happiness split her lips with a smile. "Three positive pregnancy tests ... I probably shouldn't be using *think* anymore, right?"

Ginevra's laughter coated her next words. "Definitely *not.*"

On her other side, Cara reached over to envelop August in a one-armed hug that pulled her close and felt like *love.* "Is this a new thing? How long have you—"

"So new I haven't even told Beni."

Her mother-in-law's embrace didn't loosen up even a little bit. "Not even *hinted*?"

"I started to figure it out right as I was leaving for here. He was rushing, too. It just ... didn't seem like the right time. And we're both busy, you know? I never stop with my job, and he's always going from one thing to the next with the Out—"

"Mmm," Cara interjected, stopping August before she could blurt out the name of the criminal organization her husband joined. She was still learning how to be the mob wife she needed to be for Beni. Sometimes, it wasn't easy. "That will keep a man on his feet and running for a long time. It doesn't get easier, I'm afraid. They simply learn how to manage it better."

August released a hard sigh. "At first I thought maybe this—a baby—would make things worse. We're already stretched thin ... sometimes we're spending weeks away from one another. But I'm *so* happy, too. Scared to death, but happy."

Cara hugged her tighter.

August *really* needed that.

Even Ginevra joined in, their laughter coloring up the park and ripping away all of August's worries. For the moment, anyway.

"It'll be great," Cara assured.

"It will," Ginevra agreed.

Yeah.

A part of August knew that was true. Of course, she did. How could it not be wonderful and perfect? A child made from love with the man of her dreams?

Now, she just had to tell him.

But *how*?

And when?

34.

Two weeks later ...

THE gun run took longer than anyone expected. A common hazard of their business, unfortunately. Beni wasn't even able to get word to his wife that he would be gone for a week longer than he originally said because once the run started, everyone's phones were confiscated in place of safe devices that couldn't be traced back to anyone working with smugglers. By the time he had been able to contact his wife, Beni was almost home.

Not that August seemed to mind.

Reason number one hundred why he adored his wife beyond measure.

Despite her anger, before he left because he hadn't been able to keep his promise about the New York trip, that had all seemed to go away the second he stepped inside their Melrose home. In fact, he barely remembered anything between the front door and where they found themselves in a sweaty, tangled, breathless mess on the couch.

Shit.

They hadn't even closed the blinds.

Yet, Beni couldn't find it in himself to care as he had the best view of his wife on top of him, her brown skin damp with sweat, and those dark eyes of hers locked on his stare while she rode him to *heaven*. Total fucking bliss. Every swivel of her hips tested his control. Each time she lifted on his cock and slammed right back down had air rushing out of his lungs before he sucked it right back in like it might be his last breath.

"Fuck, you look ... *look at you*," he groaned.

August had a way about her when she was fucking him. It was in the way the corner of her lip lifted; a daring smirk that said *I know* without ever actually saying a word. It was how she would bite her lip, show her teeth, and tease him with nothing more than a look. She loved being on top. *Craved* control. He swore it was because she liked to make him lose his whenever she had the chance to do so.

She got off on it.

He kind of liked that.

His wife was perfect.

Sexy as fuck.

And he was the lucky asshole to have her.

Beni knew, trust that.

As the telltale tremors started to work their way over his wife's shoulders and down her spine, Beni knew she was close to coming *again*. Oh, this wasn't their first round. Hell, it wasn't even the second. It sure as fuck wasn't going to be the last, either. Not if he had any say about it.

Which was why when he knew she was going to come again, and *quick*, he lifted his back up from the couch, grabbed that tiny waist of hers, and pushed her down to the cushions. Her low whimper—he knew that meant her orgasm had been taken away—had him chuckling.

Pulling his cock from her sopping pussy, he was able to turn her around on the couch so that she was bent over the arm. With his hands tight to her ass, spreading the plump roundness wide, so she could really feel him stretch her wide, he had to hold himself back from pounding into her all over again.

Instead, he was down on all fours.

Face between her thighs.

Eating every inch of her.

He loved the way she whined.

How she moaned.

And *shook*.

Every flick of his tongue against her most sensitive areas had August backing into him for even more. There

157

wasn't an ounce of shame in his woman when she was getting what she wanted from him, and he loved that, too.

Pinching her clit lightly while his tongue teased the spot between her slit and her ass, he murmured, "Are you gonna come for me, babe? Give me that honey?"

"*Beni.*"

Her breathy moans made his dick ache. So much so that all he could think about was getting her pussy nice and tight when she came and slipping his dick in good and slow to finally find some relief that would soon follow.

Yep.

As soon as she came.

"I'm gonna—"

August's words cut off at the same time Beni felt her pussy pulse against his tongue. He wasted no fucking time straightening up behind her and getting his cock lined up to her slit. And *yes*, she was all snug and hot and *soaked* when he worked his length into her clenching sex. Her orgasm milked his cock in the best way possible, drawing a thick moan of approval from him when he was finally seated balls-deep inside her.

For a second, he held them like that. Tight while she panted through an orgasm. *Together.* The way he always wanted them to be, really. If only life would allow him to spend all of his hours and days buried in his wife's cunt.

Wouldn't that be beautiful?

For now, he'd take this.

It was great, too.

"Hold on," he uttered through clenched teeth.

She did, those manicured nails of hers dragging lines over the arm of their leather sofa when he started pounding into her hard from behind. Every slap of his hips against her ass while his fingers left behind red indentations from his grip when he yanked her body back into his thrusts made the prettiest art on her skin.

He liked seeing his marks.

Marking *her.*

Only he got to do that.

Even though he had managed to maintain some semblance of control before, now Beni was entirely losing it. All it took was August's soft whispers, urging him to come inside her, while her pussy continued to flex with the aftershocks of her orgasm, and he was a goner.

He lost his load embarrassingly fast.

His queen did that for him.

Every time, too.

Pulling back until the head of his dick slipped out of her pussy, Beni hissed air through his teeth as he watched her sex clench until his milky cum started to spill out of her pussy. *That* was probably the best thing to watch.

Ever.

"Fuck, that's hot," he muttered, still trying to catch his breath and wetting his dry lips at the same time. "Now let's go have a shower and do it again, yeah?"

August laughed. "Give me a second to breathe."

"Just one, right?"

"*Beni.*"

His hand smacked down hard on her right ass cheek, earning him another one of her sexy moans. "Fine—you get *one* second."

"Thanks."

"Second is up."

Peeking over her shoulder, August grinned a lazy, pleased smile. "You're something else. You *really* are."

"I know. You love it."

"And *you*. Too much, probably."

"Just enough, I think," he returned.

Her observation of him turned softer as she asked, "Beni?"

"Yeah, babe?"

"I'm pregnant."

The shock that coursed through him couldn't be adequately described. Those certainly were not the words he expected to hear while she was leaking his seed, and his dick was still semi-hard. Of course, he'd thought about *that* moment ... the one when she finally gave him the kind of news he had always wanted.

Because kids were a part of his dreams.

Just like she was.

"*What?*" he asked, still not sure he'd heard her right.

"Yeah. I found out the day I went to New York, and then when I was there the last day ... I was having some cramps, I got paranoid. Mom and I went to the clinic just to get everything checked out. They found two embryos. So—"

"Twins."

Because *of course.*

Why wouldn't it be two?

Not one of his brothers had twins yet despite the oddity clearly being in their genetics. Despite the fact science said twins *wasn't* something you could pass on genetically, he didn't believe that was the case when they could literally trace twins back in their family for generations. And not just *any* kind of twin, but identical twins. *He* was the lucky fuck to pull the card first between all his brothers and that just made it *so much better.*

Beni wasn't sure if August took his silence as fear or panic, but her nervous laughter had his own starting to bubble, too.

Whenever his wife started to get nervous, she also rambled. "I'm sorry, I thought if I told you after we had sex then you wouldn't freak out and—"

"I'm not freaking out. I'm *not.* I'm so happy."

And he was.

So much.

He wanted that to be clear before anything else.

"*So fucking happy,*" he told her, leaning down to lay kiss after kiss across her sweaty back and then up to her neck and over her grinning cheek, too. "*God*, I love you. We're gonna have ... *babies.*"

August was still smiling. "Yeah, we're gonna have

babies, Beni."
It was a little terrifying.
It was also *everything*.

35.

Seven months later …

THREE-and-a-half-year-old Marcus Gian—though everybody in the family just called the boy *Marc*—lifted his head from where it had been resting against August's stomach. Her swell was now beyond the *comfortable* point.

She barely slept more than a couple of hours at a time before she needed to find a better position. She peed every twenty minutes because her two baby girls seemed to think a fun game was bouncing on their mother's bladder. And she was past the point of looking cute in maternity clothes. Not that it stopped her from trying.

"Are you sure?" Marc asked.

For a kid that hadn't even started preschool yet, he was terribly smart. Quick on his little feet, too. There wasn't a member of the Guzzi family that hadn't learned yet to be careful about what they said around Marcus Gian because the kid repeated *everything*. To perfect precision. Sometimes it was a little freaky how smart he was, but she loved her nephew to death. More than words could explain.

"I'm sure there are only two babies in there," she told him.

Marc pursed his lips, reminding her so much of his father but also *her* husband considering Bene was Beni's identical twin. And if there was anything notable about Marc beyond his young intelligence, it was the fact that he looked so much like his father and held many of the Guzzi men traits. From the way he quirked up an eyebrow when he didn't believe someone to how he laughed.

He was a Guzzi boy.

Through and through.

"Really?" he asked. "Because I think there's more. Maybe … three."

At that, he held up three fingers.

August blinked. "*Three*?"

"Four?"

The boy opened his arms wide over her stomach, his actions saying what his words were not.

"Okay, that's enough of that," Bene said, plucking his son away from August with an apologetic smile her way. "He's still trying to figure out this whole baby in the belly thing, Aug. Sorry."

She shrugged. "It's okay."

And it was.

She wasn't offended.

Besides, the kid wasn't actually wrong. She felt as huge as she looked in her final weeks of pregnancy. With only four weeks left to go, she was now just looking forward to reaching the end of this journey and holding her girls in her arms.

Next to her on the chaise where she had decided to take her dinner instead of at the large table with the rest of the family—their week-long visit was coming to an end soon—Beni shot her a knowing grin. "You don't look *that* huge."

"Just a little huge, right?"

Her husband didn't hesitate to lean across the chaise, his hand coming to rest at the top of her swell, while his mouth sought hers in a slow kiss that had August turning warm all over with every hungry sweep of his lips.

"You are *perfect*," he murmured into their kiss.

Well …

How could she argue with that?

Then, that warm sensation that had spread through her body focused between her legs. Except it was a *rush*. Or maybe gush would have been a better description.

August made a high-pitch squeak as she pulled away from Beni's next kiss. "Beni?"

"Hmm?"

"My water just broke."

Chaos ensued in the Guzzi mansion.

Because of course, it did.

• • •

Lea and Lila Guzzi came into the world on a mid-October evening, in a Canadian hospital, with their entire family waiting just down the hall to greet them. August's mother and father made it *just in time*.

They were five pounds each. Healthy as could be despite being a little early. The perfect mix of her and Beni with hazy dark eyes and black curls.

She was exhausted.

Pregnancy had *nothing* on birth.

But her world was wonderful.

Right.

Everything she wanted.

MARCUS & CELLA: PART 5

36.

Marcus

"HOW did we manage to get your parents, *my* parents, one of your brothers, and mine all in the same place today?" Cella asked at Marcus's right. "Sucks that Ren and Lucia are out of town … I'll call Liliana later to tell her, too, I guess. But hey, we didn't do too bad, did we?"

"No, we didn't."

"But how did we do it?"

His chuckle overtook the noise coming from the speaker in the car, and the man broadcasting the terrible traffic they would soon face coming into New York City. Not that it was anything new or he expected anything less. One could always count on traffic being absolute shit in Manhattan. No matter what.

"Luck," he replied.

Cella quirked a brow at that. "*Luck*?"

"I did have to threaten Corrado … but that was mostly for him to behave and less about making sure he showed up. We don't need his attitude today, do we?"

In the passenger seat of his BMW, Cella smiled in that sweet, knowing way of hers. "He can't help that he goes into his moods."

"He can help it today."

"*Marcus.*"

He only shrugged in reply; his unspoken *I said what I said* clear in the action. He meant it, too.

She could be understanding and sympathetic if she wanted when it came to his brother and Corrado's … *moods*, as Cella put it. Marcus, on the other hand, planned for this day to go off without a single hitch in the plans. Including any attitude from Corrado that might do nothing more than make Cella frown.

She wouldn't be doing anything but smiling while she delivered the news of their pregnancy to their families. The only thing on her mind would be the *happiness* of it all. Nothing less. He was quite aware that Cella was already nervous about this day, the dinner, and the announcement in general.

They were unmarried … practically unheard of for men and women like them that came from the backgrounds and families they did. Not to mention, he was sure there would be a lot of questions bounced back from their families about when they planned to get married or living arrangements because they were still in two different countries. Questions were to be expected. It was still nerve-racking to answer them when, for the moment, they didn't have every single answer.

But they still wanted to share their news.

And they were *adults*.

Fuck the rest.

They would figure it out.

At the same time, he was sure it was going to be fine. Everyone would be happy. There wasn't any reason to think that *wouldn't* be the case so whenever Cella dared to let one of her worries slip, that was exactly what he told her.

Everything would be *fine*.

"I think *some* of them—my mom, mostly," Marcus grumbled lower when Cella shot a glance his way, "probably has an idea about what we're going to tell them today, anyway."

"Why?"

"Not because I said! I didn't tell *any* secrets. I promised."

The new voice from the backseat had Marcus grinning wide when he peered into the reflection of the rearview mirror. In her safety seat, Tiffany beamed back as proud as could be.

"Right, Marcus?" she asked.

"Right, you promised," he agreed. "And you've been great about keeping the secret." Even Cella turned a bit in her seat, putting her hand over her eyes to shield the glare of the late August sun coming in through the window. "You were perfect about it, baby."

As always, when Tiffany was praised, she soaked that up like a sponge in water. Every last drop of it until she beamed in her seat, the pink in her cheeks matching the color of her summer dress and the bow in her blonde ponytail. There was nothing that kid liked more than being told she had done a good job.

Next to him, Cella cleared her throat to gain his attention as she shifted her hand to the side of her face so that her daughter couldn't see what she mouthed to Marcus. "To be fair, we've also kept her *very* busy for the last month."

He had to hold back the laughter.

She wasn't wrong.

They had spent a lot of time searching for a doctor in New York that was also willing to work with a doctor in Toronto, as Cella would need physicians in both countries for a portion of the pregnancy if not all of it. At least until they figured out where they wanted the twins born and whether it would be possible.

Cella also had work to handle and *clients*. Marcus had *famiglia* business that never ended. Add in to all of that trying to make time for each other and getting Tiffany ready for the upcoming school year … well, it was a lot. They didn't stop moving or doing something, for that matter.

Not that he complained. Ever. Because he didn't. Whatever it took for them to be together and happy, Marcus was willing to do it. In fact, he would be the first to step up and do it.

Cella only needed to ask.

He made that clear.

In no way did Marcus think everything would be easy

for him and Cella. Especially not as they navigated the territory ahead of them with the pregnancy, getting married, *moving* ... more. But he was willing to do it. He would make it all happen for her.

Anything to be with her.

That's what love was.

Right?

As though Cella could read his mind, and he believed that she could sometimes, she leaned across the space between their seats to press a quick kiss to the side of his cheek. It was really all she could afford on the busy freeway as he couldn't take his gaze away from the road for too long to spare very much more.

Not that it stopped him from trying.

He turned to catch her lips with his own. Fast and fleeting. Her silken mouth barely grazed his, and he didn't even get a proper taste of her with how fast it had been. And yet, it was still perfect, the imprint of her smile lingered on his own, and her heavenly perfume coating every breath he took was more than enough to sedate him.

For now, anyway.

Marcus would get more from her later.

He always did.

The tips of her manicured nails teased the line of his cleanly-shaven jaw as the little girl in the backseat asked, "Are we there yet?"

"Almost," Marcus and Cella lied in unison.

Not even close.

All in all, Tiffany was a pretty good car kid, though. She didn't mind long drives, but if they told her the truth then she would ask that same question every five minutes until they finally arrived. Nobody wanted that. Not even Tiff herself.

"Back to your mom," Cella said. "What makes you think she knows?"

Ah, yeah.

He forgot about that.

Cella was a good distraction.

Marcus drummed his fingers to the steering wheel, considering the conversation he had with his mother earlier that week where she mentioned the dinner in New York *and* asked about their surprise announcement. Not that he gave her anything when she asked. Certainly, no details that ruined the pregnancy surprise. Cara's simple but frank *it's finally your turn, Marcus* made him think his mother knew what they were coming to tell everyone before they even said it.

"Because she just does," Marcus said. "She's my ma ... she knows everything."

That made Cella laugh.

"Fair enough. Moms just know."

Marcus was also wrong.

From the backseat, Tiffany asked again, "Are you sure we're not there yet?"

37.

Cella

THANKFULLY, Tiffany only asked another five more times if they had arrived or not by the time they did actually arrive at Cella's father's restaurant in Manhattan. *Kids.* If nothing else could keep a person entertained and on their toes, a kid could certainly do it. Cella's daughter definitely did, anyway. She loved Tiffany for it, too.

Unfortunately, when they did arrive at the restaurant, Cella's morning sickness—that *never* seemed to make an appearance during morning hours—decided that was the time to make itself known. She opted to sip on water and breathe through her nose for a few minutes instead of getting out of the vehicle right away. Standing only made the nausea way worse.

Her doctor, the one in New York that she had seen more than once since finding out she was pregnant, said women carrying a multiples pregnancy often had bad morning sickness. Worse than normal.

Lucky her.

She watched Marcus wrangle Tiffany out of the backseat and greet the waiting enforcer at the front of the restaurant. Then, her daughter grabbed the hand of the large man and headed inside the business. The familiar cars parked in the reserved spots told her that their family was already there and ready to get the dinner started.

Waiting on them.

Finally, Marcus made his way back to the passenger side of the car. Wind from the street wrapped around her legs, making the flowy skirt of her dress blow wildly when he opened the door for her. She tried to admire the sight of Marcus in his pressed, black slacks and silk button-down that he had rolled up to his elbows. The dark dusting of

171

hair that peeked out of the buttons he'd left undone at his throat disappeared beneath his shirt, and the way his Adam's apple bobbed with his swallow was a teasing distraction for Cella.

Then again, everything beautiful and sinful about this man was a distraction to her. One she was happy to chase whenever, wherever. Only Marcus did that for her.

Usually, he went for his staple three-piece suits, but the summer heat had him opting for something less heavy, constricting, and hot. She didn't blame him a bit. Besides, his silk shirts allowed her a great view of the definition in his back and arms. She certainly wasn't going to complain about that.

Even if right then all she wanted to do was lose her lunch all over his shined, leather loafers. Knowing Marcus, he would probably just smile and tell her that was okay, too.

"Any better?" he asked.

Cella laughed weakly. "Define *better*."

Marcus made a face. "Well, if I don't get us in there someone is going to come out here and ask *why*, sweetheart."

Right.

Cella didn't want their news to be ruined for their waiting family because her morning sickness decided to be a bitch that day.

"One more minute?" she asked him.

Marcus leaned into the car and pressed a soft kiss to her forehead, murmuring, "Sure, whatever you need."

With him close, the summer warmth hugging her tight, and fresh air blowing through the car, Cella did start to feel better as the seconds ticked by. She didn't need the full minute before she was able to step out of the vehicle with Marcus's help. Turning to face the side entrance of the restaurant, the same one Tiffany had just taken with the family's enforcer, Cella exhaled the stress that had been resting low in her belly like a heavy weight.

Even if she hadn't acknowledged it.

It *was* there.

Well, not anymore.

This was a good day. The *perfect* moment to celebrate their pregnancy with their families. Nothing was going to ruin that, but especially not any fear she felt when there really wasn't much reason for her to feel it.

"Let's share the good news," she told Marcus.

His sexy grin glinted in the daylight. "Let's do it, Cella."

• • •

Cella had to give her daughter credit because it was due. Despite having almost ten minutes alone with her grandparents and everyone else waiting for Cella and Marcus inside the restaurant, Tiffany managed to keep quiet about the surprise. Even though she was probably the most excited of them all to share the news that she was going to be a big sister, she didn't.

By the time Cella and Marcus took their seats at the large table in the private dining section, everyone was already looking their way.

Waiting.

Expecting …

Wondering, she bet.

Once they were past the usual greetings from everyone, and each person had their moment to say hello, give a hug or a kiss, as was the Italian way, Cella and Marcus took their seats on either side of Tiffany. The conversation at the table continued, quieter than it had been when they first entered the space as it seemed like the attention from their families was now all on them.

"Where's the food?" Cella asked, refusing to acknowledge the curious gazes observing her and Marcus. They could wait a few moments more, surely. It wouldn't kill any of them. "I thought we were doing a buffet?"

"We are. Food's coming," her father said.

"We sent for it once we knew you guys had arrived," her mother added.

Her parents sat at the head of the table. Marcus's parents sat at the other end. His brother—with Corrado's large family in tow—sat across from them while John, his wife, and their kids sat in the chairs next to Cella, Marcus, and Tiff.

The whole table was full.

"We *do* have an announcement, right?" Corrado asked across the table. "Because that's what I was told and—"

"Quiet," Marcus murmured, pointing a finger his brother's way.

"What?"

"It's the wedding, right?" Siena asked at Cella's far-right. "We're finally going to get a date for a wedding, I bet."

"About time," John added, shooting his sister a smirk. "I'm just saying, Cella."

And just like that, a wave of chatter moved from person to person at the table. It didn't slow or stop, and each new person had something different to add. Cella let her family—and Marcus's—do their usual thing.

Nothing new to see.

They were still loud.

Nosy.

Of course.

"If everyone is quite finished," came the soft, amused voice of Cara Guzzi at the far end of the table where she sat with her husband. The two stared Cella and Marcus's way; they hadn't joined the chatter with the rest of the table. "I would like to hear the surprise. Wouldn't you, Gian?"

Next to her, Gian nodded. "I would."

"I was hoping to eat first," Cella said, only half teasing, as Marcus leaned in closer to her by bending over the back of Tiffany's chair between them. His fingers tickled her side with a soft touch while he kissed the shell of her ear at the same time. "Then we could get around to the

174

surprise."

"Just tell them," Marcus urged in her ear.

"Why don't *you*?"

"Or we could let Tiff."

At the mere mention of her name, Tiffany popped up brighter than ever in her chair. "Yes, I will! *Can I*?"

The laughter from their families colored up the table. Cella shot Marcus a silent question when their eyes met. He shrugged in response. It seemed like an okay to her.

"Go ahead, baby," Cella told Tiff as Marcus straightened in his chair again. "Tell them the surprise!"

Tiffany didn't wait one second before belting out, "I'm gonna have *two* little brothers … or sisters!"

"And we're getting married," Cella added quickly, "but the surprise was more the babies."

Silence coated the table.

Before it exploded with happiness.

Chairs scraped the floor as their families left their seats. Before Cella knew what happened, she was surrounded by her mother and father, brother, and her in-laws. Their congratulations, hugs, and kisses rained down until she was sure that she couldn't take one more second of it. Yet, she did. And she loved it, too.

"You owe me a grand, Gian," Lucian said.

"How so?" replied her soon-to-be father-in-law. "I said a wedding. *You* said a pregnancy. We were both right. It's even."

"Pregnancy was first. A win is a win, man."

Gian grinned, asking, "But is it? Because I remember Marcus mentioning that he had come to have a chat with you not too long ago … why didn't *you* pick marriage?"

Lucian smirked right back. "I never pick a sure bet, Gian. Accept your loss."

Chuckles passed between the men at the table, including Marcus beside her, as their families retook their seats. Finally, the food started to come in, too. Cella would have been more than happy to focus on getting some grub—she was *always* hungry, now—but a question from her mother stopped her from reaching for the bowl of bread that the server sat down within her arm's reach.

"When is the wedding?" Jordyn asked her. "Before, or after the babies are born?"

"Before," Marcus said.

At the same time, Cella answered, "We don't know."

The two of them turned to face each other.

More laughter skipped down the table.

Marcus cocked a brow, saying, "We'll get back to you guys on that one. Right, babe?"

Cella grinned. "Right."

One thing at a time.

It's how they dealt with everything.

Shit.

It worked.

38.

"DADDY?"

It didn't matter how many times Tiffany called Marcus her daddy, it still hit him in the chest every single time. Like a kick that he couldn't avoid, it smacked him hard with the weight of what it meant to be that man for her, and he was as honored as he was determined not to fuck it up in some way.

She only said it now when it was just them in private, or with her mother. She did sometimes refer to him as her dad to others when people asked but for the most part, Tiffany was still testing the waters in that regard.

Marcus didn't mind.

She could take all the time she needed. He would be there, willing to answer to whatever title she wanted to call him whether that was her dad, daddy, or that guy who loved her mother. He was fine no matter what. The choice was all hers.

"Yeah?" Marcus asked, leaning in the bedroom doorway.

Instead of making the long drive back to Toronto, they opted to stay the rest of the weekend in Rochester at Cella's place. Though it sometimes made work hard for Marcus—even if he wouldn't tell Cella that—he never said one thing or another about his place in Toronto or staying here with her when she wanted. He was up for whatever.

Still.

Tucked under her pink bedding, Tiffany's questions shone through in her stare. She had done well at the dinner with their families. For a kid that needed to ask as much as she liked to talk, she had allowed the adults to have their conversations without really butting in for most of the

177

dinner. And he was grateful, but he wasn't surprised she was ready to talk now, either.

"Is Mommy done?"

"Nope. Still on the phone," he said. "She'll be in when she's done. Okay?"

He didn't bother to explain Cella was on a call with a client who had been pressing her for a final deadline for two weeks. It wasn't like Tiffany would understand, anyway. And he hadn't hesitated to get the girl ready for bed and pull out a bedtime story to read when Cella got the call earlier. He stepped in where she couldn't and filled in where she needed him to. She didn't even need to ask him to do it.

He just did it.

Wasn't that what parents did? What *love* was?

Tiffany didn't mind, either.

"Well, I have a question," Tiffany said, raising her blonde brows high like she expected Marcus to reply in the only appropriate way.

Which he knew was, "And what question is that, love?"

Her smile said he was right.

"When you and my mom get married," she said, squinting upward at the canopy over her bed as though she was seriously considering her next words, "does that mean we're all going to live together?"

That was not the question he expected. And yet ... It was an easy answer, he thought.

Even though they practically lived together anyway between New York and Toronto, it also wasn't official. He bet—for Tiffany, mostly—she saw the clear distinction between the home they called Marcus's house, and the place in Rochester where she lived with Cella before he ever came along. And to her, that distinction meant they weren't living in the same home.

Not like other people did.

She wasn't wrong.

"Well, yes," Marcus replied.

"Oh," Tiffany replied. "But … *here?*"

Ah, there it was.

He heard it that time.

The hesitance.

"Probably Toronto," Marcus said, "and not here. But you like it there, don't you? You could pick a whole new school or even go to the one Maria goes to if you wanted. Which means you would already have a friend. And you'll have lots of family there from my side. Lots of Guzzis. I know it would be a change, and it's not like … here. But it could be after a while. It could be home, too."

Tiffany let out a big breath.

Marcus smiled, waiting her out.

"I guess," she finally said. "I *do* like Toronto. And we'll come back to visit lots and lots, right? We're still coming back here to—"

"As much as you want, no worries."

Or as much as was possible.

He seriously doubted the Marcello family would give him much of a choice when it came to them spending a reasonable amount of time with Cella and Tiffany. As it was, if Lucian thought his daughter and granddaughter hadn't come around enough, the man didn't hesitate to let Marcus know that needed to be corrected. *ASAP.*

Marcus respected it.

Mostly.

"And I think," Marcus added, "that when we do move you and your mom to Toronto, it won't be to *my* house that I live in now."

"*No?* Where?"

He grinned. "A *new* house. With a bigger bedroom for you. A theater room where we could do movies. Probably a swimming pool, too."

Shit, he wanted the whole deal. A mansion with a couple of wings, just because. Like the one he grew up in, even.

If Marcus was going to finally go all out when it came to

179

his adult life, including getting married, he might as well settle right down into it as well. Like buying the home of his wife's dreams that she could decorate to her heart's desire.

Why the hell not?

Tiffany sunk back into her blankets, the expression on her face telling him she was far happier about the idea of a move than she had been minutes before. "And a puppy, too?"

"What?"

"Could I have a puppy at the new house?"

Marcus laughed, unable to stop it even when he replied, "You know what, Tiff, we will certainly see what I can do about that."

The littlest love of his life eyed him from her mound of pillows. "That wasn't a yes."

Smart kid.

Then, Tiffany smiled when she added, "But that wasn't a no, either."

Marcus pointed a finger her way and winked. "Exactly."

And with kids, sometimes it was all about the compromise. Even if he knew Tiffany wasn't the type of kid to forget about this in a few months. That was fine with him.

39.

"DID I hear you promise Tiffany a *puppy*?"

At least, Cella thought, Marcus had the decency to look slightly ashamed when he strolled into her home office.

"Maybe," he returned as his attention drifted to the phone on her desk. "Weren't you on the phone with a client? Why are you eavesdropping on my conversations with Tiff, anyway?"

Despite what his reply suggested, there was no heat to his words. Thing was, Cella really did trust Marcus with her daughter. He'd proven himself capable, responsible, and loving on more than one occasion with Tiffany. He never crossed a line; not even the suggestion of it.

She also trusted her daughter felt safe enough that if something made her uncomfortable, she would speak up about it. She always had before. Even if it was just saying that she didn't like sharing a bathroom with a boy because of all his *boy* things, as Tiffany had put it.

Mostly, Cella figured that was just so her daughter could have easier access to all the pretty things—like her mom's makeup and perfume—when they switched around who used what bathrooms.

"Nice try."

Marcus chuckled deeply. "Had to give it a shot. You miss a hundred percent of the shots you don't take, right? That's what I was told once. And technically, it wasn't a yes or no on the puppy. Nothing firm. What, are you against pets? Wouldn't have taken you for the type, love."

Mmhmm.

She heard how he tried to switch that around on her at the end. But she also wasn't that easy to trick, and a puppy would be a lot of work.

"I'm against more work or responsibility getting shoveled onto my plate than I already have to deal with," Cella explained, shrugging under the silkiness of the robe she had thrown on earlier as she readied for bed. "How are we going to do this, Marcus?"

That had him quirking a brow.

She cocked one right back.

"Do what?" he asked.

Cella widened her arms, hoping he got the point at her rather *wide* gesture. When he didn't seem to catch on, she let out a breath of frustration before saying, "*Everything*, you know? Getting married. This pregnancy. Oh, and now we're apparently going to start talking about *moving*, too. And if I trust what I heard you telling Tiff, it won't be just moving to your place. It'll be buying a whole *house*. Like that's not a lot of—"

"Cella."

She ignored his quiet hum of her name and how it sounded both amused and calming coming out of his mouth. Instead, she continued to rush right ahead with her ranting because that felt better for the moment. "I suspect you're going to want to do that before the babies get here, too. I also need to find a *new* office space for my business because if I am moving to Toronto, then so is my company. But let's not forget the client I was just talking to that—even though I *should* cancel the contract because it would clear up my time a bit—I don't actually want to. I was looking forward to that job."

"Cella … *babe*, hey, are you done?"

Her eyes snapped upward from where she had focused her stare on the buttons of his shirt while she rambled her way through the mess of thoughts and feelings that hadn't left her alone for most of the past month. His conversation with Tiffany might have brought it to the surface where she was willing to say something, but that didn't mean it was a *new* thing.

None of this was new.

All this stress?

It didn't leave Cella alone.

"Am I *done*?" she asked, every word measured.

Marcus must have heard the warning there because as he crossed the room with a laugh and his arms open wide, he said, "Sorry—bad choice of words. I just meant, could I step in and say a few things now or do you need more time to get out … the rest of the lovely mess in your head?"

She was stuck on how he called her a *lovely* mess. Or did he mean her anxiety and stress that she had just word vomited to a pile while he watched?

What did it even matter?

Cella didn't have the opportunity to ask either way because before she could even blink, Marcus had closed the space between them, and had her wrapped in his embrace in the next second. His strong arms tightened around her as she buried her face into the crook of his neck. Dragging in a deep breath, his scent came with it, calming her further. The soft *thump-thump-thump* of his heart beating against her own chest when they were tight together only soothed her further.

That's what this man did for her.

In *every* way.

Even when life was crazy.

He was solid ground while the world crumbled around her. An unmovable pillar in the hurricane of life. The safe-haven she could run to whenever she needed him no matter the reason.

Marcus kissed the top of Cella's head before murmuring, "I was going to tell you all the solutions I have ready for these problems … but really, I only have one question. Can I ask it?"

Pulling back from him just enough that she could tip her head and stare up at Marcus who grinned at the sight of her own smile, Cella said, "Ask it, then."

Not that she had any idea what he would ask.

He always managed to surprise her.

"What if I could make it *all* happen? What would you say then?"

She arched a brow. "All of it?"

"With little to no effort on your part. Or none that will take away from the things you want or need to do, and the time you have for yourself and us. What if I could make it happen?"

She didn't know if that was possible.

Marcus's sexy grin didn't falter the longer she stayed silent, considering his words. He was always so confident; it was one of the things she adored about him the most. There was a fine line between confidence and cocky arrogance, but Marcus walked it well. Better than most.

"Well?" he urged.

"I would say yes. If you could make it all happen—everything—before the babies were born, then yes. I just don't think that's—"

Cella didn't get another word out before Marcus kissed her. Bruising and beautifully *good*, too. So swift, it took her breath right from her lungs. She lost herself in the hard strokes of his lips that urged hers to open for him until his tongue was sliding along her own, dominating even the way she responded to his kiss. The same way he took control between them in bed. His kiss was the same and she *adored* it.

Everything.

All of him.

She loved it all.

"All I needed was the *yes*," Marcus murmured against her trembling lips after he had slowed their kiss. "And now I'm taking you to bed. Be quiet on the way—someone may still be awake. Does that sound good to you?"

That time, her yes came easier.

How could it not?

Cella wasn't sure *how* she managed to keep quiet even after they were hidden inside the safety of the master bedroom … but she did. Well, maybe that was because once Marcus had her stripped naked and on her knees in the middle of her bed, he stuffed her panties into her mouth to muffle the noises that he drew from her lips as he worked her body to heaven.

Higher and higher.

She loved him between her thighs.

The way he held her body down with his strong hands and ate her until her hips strained against his hold, and her heart felt like it was going to explode. He knew every way to drive her crazy with nothing more than the flick of his tongue against her pussy. There was something about the way he moaned, the thick sound coming off appreciative when he had that tarte taste of her heavy on his tongue.

And when he finally made her come? Then slid his cock in deep? *God.* He fucked her with slow but hard pumps that took away what remained of her sense and sensibility.

Yeah.

Cella didn't regret saying yes to Marcus. Not for a second.

She never did.

40.

Marcus

WHILE his brother's voice droned through the speakers in the car, Marcus's mind was somewhere else entirely. Somewhere in a soft bed where he could still feel Cella's silky thighs trembling under his grasp as he widened them to accommodate him slipping between her legs. Somewhere that her moans when he filled her full of his cock still echoed in his mind long after she'd reached her orgasm, and she was urging him to chase his own.

He could feel how her inner walls hugged him when he had her stretched and full. Or how her arousal coated his tongue, and the flavor remained even after he'd fucked her crazy. And then the way salt made it even better when he kissed her damp skin.

Somewhere else …

Somewhere better.

Where he could taste her again.

Smell her sex.

Fuck her.

At the end of the day, Marcus still put on a good show to the rest of the public. In his suits, with his hair combed back in place, an expensive watch ticking away at his wrist, and his shoes always shined, he *looked* like the very embodiment of what he was meant to be. Of what he had been *raised* to be.

The next boss.

The Guzzi king.

His father's prodigy.

In *every* way.

And yet, underneath it all, Marcus still remained a live wire wrapped up in nothing more than a good suit. He might smile and nod when needed, and he always inserted

186

his commentary into conversations at the right time that he was expected to, but in his mind ... the one place no one but him could see and be, well, there he was much different.

Baser.

Carnal.

Raw.

Safe.

"And Mom and Dad are back, then?" Marcus asked.

"As of this morning," Chris replied. "Yes."

"Perfect."

"But where are *you*?"

That made Marcus smirk. "I know, I know. I should be on my way back to Toronto today as well, but—"

"I can move some shit around," his brother interjected. "It's a little easier when you give me a heads up about it, though."

Fair point.

"I'll make note of that," Marcus returned.

But he knew Chris heard good and well what he didn't say. He didn't have to be accommodating to *anyone* as the boss. Everyone else had to accommodate him now. That was perfectly fucking fine with him. Even if the rest of his men were still learning what it meant to serve the new head of the family.

"I do have something else I need you to do for me, though," Marcus said, needing to finish up the conversation with his brother. The woman who had come to park alongside his vehicle in the lot gave him a wave from her car that he returned. His lunch date had arrived, and it was time to move onto the next part of his current task—giving Cella what she needed and wanted like he promised to do. He was nothing if not a man of his word. "If you're up for it, of course."

"When am I not?" Chris replied.

Marcus laughed under his breath.

Well ...

It wasn't like Chris had a choice.

"You know the realtor I had been meeting with before coming to New York?"

"Laurie, yeah. Dad's favorite."

Marcus's, too.

Was that by accident?

Not likely.

"Yeah, her. Get her on the phone. Before supper, I want an email with all the details, photos, and whatever else she wants to send about the property she had approached me with a while back."

"You were looking at a place?"

Marcus grinned at the tone his brother took on. "Are you offended that you weren't aware I have a life outside of the things we discuss, or ...?"

"I mean, I didn't know you were looking to buy a new house. That's all."

"Not just another house. A *home*, actually."

Chris sighed. "Right, I get it. I'll get on the phone with the realtor, too."

"Thanks, man. Now, I've got ... other things to do, so."

"Right, right. Later, boss."

Marcus hung up the call without his own goodbye. Not that his brother would expect anything less from him now. They all had their roles to fill in their business, and he had chosen the one he wanted to play just like Chris had decided on his own as well. They did what they needed to do. Simple as that.

By the time Marcus stepped out of his vehicle, the woman from the car beside his had also exited hers to greet him with a hand stuck out for a shake.

"Marcus Guzzi, right?" she asked.

He nodded, shaking her hand but quickly letting it go once he was satisfied. "I am—and you are Marilyn Cooper. Wedding planner *extraordinaire*. Or that's what everyone has told me when I asked who could get something like this done in a short amount of time."

The green-eyed, sprite of a woman with dark, spiky hair grinned like she was pleased *and* proud. It really was funny and terrifying how easily and quickly Marcus could pull things together when he needed to. It helped to be rich. It also didn't hurt to have a last name like his that demanded attention and respect when he signed it to a check.

"Good to know people get it right when they talk about me," Marilyn replied.

Marcus laughed, saying, "They sure do. Are you ready to meet my fiancée? This is going to be a bit of a surprise for her."

"Oh?"

"Don't worry. She's in a good mood today. I made sure of that."

• • •

"Marcus?" Cella's entire face brightened when he walked into her Rochester office with Marilyn, the wedding planner, close behind on his heels. "I thought you were heading back to Toronto today?"

"I can afford one more day here."

Surely.

Cella rounded her desk with questions in her eyes as her attention drifted between him and the woman behind him. Marcus took his time to properly greet his fiancée before introducing the two women, however. Kissing Cella to her cheek and resting his arm along her lower back to hold her close, he always wanted her to know she was the most important thing in his world.

Or the room.

Whatever.

"Surprise," he murmured against the top of Cella's head. "I hope you didn't have any plans for lunch. I know Tiff is having a play date with her friend—I'll pick her up, so it's one less thing you have to worry about today. I thought maybe you would be trying to catch up on stuff, so this would be the best time to—"

"Bring a friend," Cella interjected.

Marcus's chuckles rocked them both. "A planner, actually. A *wedding* planner. Cella, this is—"

"Marilyn Cooper," the woman said before Marcus could, her bubbly personality showing through even more when she darted forward to offer her hand to Cella with a bright, wide smile. "I have heard *so much* about the infamous Cella Marcello and your interior designs. I can't believe I'm going to be planning your wedding. This is *crazy town*."

Cella gaped. Marcus just laughed.

"Need a minute to catch up, babe?" he asked Cella.

She nodded. "Just one or two, yeah." Peering up at him, she asked lower, "Really? A *planner*?"

"It'll be easy. No stress at all. A three-month deadline is pretty typical for my clients, if not less. You won't have to do much more than pick a dress, agree to a color scheme and theme, and show up on time, Cella. I promise."

Cella clearly heard everything the woman said, but she only looked Marcus's way when she asked, "You picked a date, then? *Three* months?"

"That's before the babies," he returned. "Which is what you wanted. And you did say yes to me making things happen if it didn't interfere with anything else, right?"

"I did say that ... now I'm wondering what else you're just waiting to pull out of your hat."

She was quick.

He wasn't done yet.

Marilyn tittered on the spot, her excitement becoming a voracious ball of energy in the office. "Is that a yes, then? Am I officially planning a wedding?"

Cella let out a soft laugh when Marcus grinned her way. "I guess yeah ... that's a yes."

As long as she kept saying yes, then he would keep making things happen.

Fair was fair.

41.

Cella

KNOWING Marcus planned to pick Tiffany up from her playdate with a friend, Cella wasn't at all surprised to walk into her kitchen after work and find the two of them laughing together. It was the rows of printed images that they had spread over the massive countertop space that made her pause in the doorway.

Even from her spot, she could see the images made up a larger picture. Of what looked to be rooms, spaces, crown molding, flooring, a garage, and so much more.

"What are you two doing?"

Tiffany didn't even look up from the photo she held. "Shopping, Ma."

"*What?*"

Marcus's dark laughter hit her square in the gut as he crossed the room to greet her first before anything else. He always did that; she had started to notice it, and she *liked* it. She loved the feeling that he made sure that she knew she was the first thing on his mind even when all she had done was walk into a room where he was too.

How did she get so lucky?

Her second chance at forever was proving to be everything she could ever want and more. Then again, she figured Marcus should take the credit for that. He certainly put in the effort to make it work with them. *Every day.*

Tipping her head back in his palms, he dotted sweet kisses across her pouty smile. "How was the rest of your day?"

"Good."

"The planner—the *plans?*"

Cella grinned. "We made some headway on things over lunch. I think she knows where to go from here with

191

different things I like, and I'll be seeing her again in a couple of weeks to go over more details."

"No stress, right?"

"*Marcus.*"

"Hmm?" he asked, smiling in that knowing way of his.

"You're amazing."

"I'm only trying a little, sweetheart."

Really?

Only a little?

She wondered what this might look like if he put one-hundred percent of his effort into it. Actually, that might be a little terrifying.

Marcus pressed closer to her, molding their chests together as his warm palms slid down her body until he had her tiny waist in his hands, and his thumbs could stroke the sides of her stomach. Where his babies grew, she knew. He was careful about never intruding on her space and body but when it was just them and things were quiet, his hands *always* found her stomach. A *very* small curve was just starting to grow there. Soon, she knew it would be huge. He still seemed to love what she had for now.

"I try to keep my word, that's all," Marcus said, showing his white teeth as he winked. "Are you happy? Is it working?"

She didn't think people knew the truth about Marcus ... something in his personality that barely anyone but perhaps those closest to him could see. For those he loved, he felt such a strong need to please them. Especially *her*. And he wanted to know he was doing it and doing it well. That's when he was most happy.

"It's working," she promised.

"Good."

"And you didn't answer my question," she added, leaning to the side to peer around him at the photos still spread out across her kitchen. Tiffany had crawled up on the island to grab a photo further down the counter.

"What is all this?"

Marcus stepped back, waving an arm wide. "Take a peek for yourself. Let me know what you think."

He kept talking as she headed for the closest countertop filled with pictures. Setting her bag aside, she reached for one that showcased the front entrance of a rather large home. The circular driveway crossed under marble pillars that supported a roof that jutted out from the front of the house. Massive double doors stained in a rich color waited just above marble stairs. The next picture was of a guesthouse. Another showcased a winding staircase.

"I thought the guest house would work well for the office spaces—it's more than large enough. The main house itself has seventeen bedrooms. That's not enough for us to find a space for a guest to sleep? We didn't need the guesthouse for *that*. Better used for you and your work, right?"

Cella moved from photo to photo, saying nothing. Marcus let her. Beside Tiffany, who was so excited to show her the photos of the room she wanted to be *her* bedroom, waited a binder that Cella hadn't seen in months … possibly even longer. She didn't need to open it up to know what was inside.

Her designs.

Things she wanted.

Ideas for her own home.

Her *someday* home.

"I thought we could hire someone," Marcus said from behind her as she reached for the binder, "to bring your vision to life without actually taking time away from what you're doing now. If you like that idea, of course. Otherwise, we could work on the new house in our time when we're able. Everything is up to us, you know?"

Cella understood, then.

She *really* got it.

The tear that slipped out of the corner of her eye didn't last long before she had wiped it away with a quick sniffle as the only proof that it had existed in the first place.

"How long have you been looking at this house?"

"The realtor sent me information about the Quebec estate a couple of weeks ago, but I mean, I've been looking for something for us for—"

"Before the pregnancy?"

"Oh, yeah. Easily. I knew where we were going, Cella. I knew what I wanted. *You*. It was just a one-step-at-a-time kind of thing. Then, the pregnancy happened. We had to change some plans around. It's nothing I can't handle."

Right.

Because he took it all on himself.

He expected nothing from her.

Nothing but love.

"And hey, if this isn't the kind of place you're interested in," he said, coming to stand at her back where he could reach alongside to move some of the photos on the counter, "then I can send back that info to the realtor, and she'll know to look elsewhere."

"But I *love* this house," Tiffany put in, making Cella laugh.

Even Marcus chuckled.

"It is beautiful, isn't it?" she asked him.

"I love it, yeah. But it's not just about *me*—"

"Except it should also be about you, Marcus. Not everything is all about me, either."

"It is in my world, babe."

The two of them stared at one another, unmoving.

He quietly added, "And if you said yes to this one, I was told any changes and designs would be done before the babies arrived. They'll come home to—"

"A home," she whispered. "*Their* home."

"Yeah."

His hands found the tiny swell of her midsection again. Everything was *right*.

"Is that another yes, then?" Marcus asked.

At this point, she wasn't sure there was another answer

she could give. He seemed to take great pride in making sure the only thing she could say was …

"That's a yes."

42.

Marcus

MARCUS hadn't expected the Quebec estate to be an almost immediate yes for Cella. He figured she would probably want to see the place first, maybe do a tour of the mansion and surrounding property as well as the guest house. Especially when his plan was to turn the place into both their home and her company's office.

He had been warned how particular Cella could be when it came to searching for a place to call their own. Apparently it took her first husband nearly two years of looking before he found the house she wanted to settle into. The Rochester house she bought after his death had been more a necessity than something she truly wanted which was why she didn't waffle long when it came to buying that property.

Nonetheless, Marcus expected some pushback.

Anything.

She surprised him by jumping into the Quebec estate wholeheartedly. At first, he worried that she was going to regret the choice to buy the property *later*. Maybe after the chaotic period of their life slowed back to a normal pace; when they weren't constantly running for appointments relating to the pregnancy, counting down the days to a wedding, *and* now working on getting a massive mansion move-in ready by the time their twins were born.

It concerned him.

That was all.

Marcus quickly realized how silly his worries were when six weeks after they finalized the purchase of the estate, and he was able to watch Cella walk through the halls of what would become their home. It was like she knew every step; each one was comforting and *familiar*. She already had a vision and a plan forming for what she wanted, and the picture she painted took hold in his mind the more she described it.

He didn't need her to say it.

Even he could feel it.

The place was *perfect*.

Everything they wanted.

All they needed.

Seventeen bedrooms. Ten bathrooms. There was more than enough space to add in the theater room he wanted. The indoor pool that had been integrated into the finished basement that also connected to the guest house through an underground hallway was great, too. Set deep in the middle of a ten-acre private, forested property that they planned to fence *and* gate in, the estate couldn't have been more perfect.

Really.

They had left Tiffany with his parents while they made the trip to the estate only because it was late, they already had a long drive the next day back to New York, and Cella wanted her to get as much rest as she could. More rest was basically the same thing Marcus wanted for *Cella*, but he figured it was better to let her just do what she wanted. Especially when she wasn't complaining about being tired despite spending the last two hours going room to room within the mansion.

"And?" came the familiar voice in Marcus's ear.

Smiling, he replied to his father on the call, "She is ... *in love*."

Gian's dark laughter matched his own. "I figured she would adore it. The place felt very ... *you and her* if you know what I mean."

"Really? I thought maybe once she saw it—I don't know, maybe she would find things that were a problem. Instead, she's just ... over the moon."

To say the least.

"Even the pickiest women will have moments where

perfect things are placed in their hands, and the only thing they can do is say thank you," his father returned. "Congratulations, Marcus, you managed to do that for her with the estate. Your mother is *dying* to go have a look, by the way. Drop off a set of keys, would you? I'm sure we can afford a weekend trip to Quebec soon for her to check it out."

Marcus nodded though his father couldn't see it. "Sure, will do."

"Tiff is great, by the way. Already sleeping."

"Speaking of sleeping."

"Hmm?"

"It's late. And a four-hour drive back. It'll be almost two in the morning by the time we get there. There's still furniture in some of the rooms, and I'm sure the blankets in the back of the car will do us fine for the night. We'll get up early and start the drive back. Probably get there around breakfast or shortly after."

"First night in your new home?"

Marcus chuckled. "Is it our home yet when we're not moving in for a few more months and—"

"It's your home, Marcus. Take a good, long look at those halls, the walls, and every single room, son … because, for the rest of your life, that's where you're working to return to each night. Those are the floors where your babies will learn to walk; the windows where they'll slap their dirty handprints to the glass."

"You think?"

"I *know*. Those walls will hear your love and absorb every word. So maybe it doesn't *look* like it will in five months or ten years—it is still your home. The heart of everything in your life. You'll remember how it started as it becomes what it was always meant to be. Watching it change and grow is the best part, I promise."

Huh.

"You know," he said to his father, "there really is something to be said for the way you're able to say things,

Papa. The *right* things. Especially for us, your boys. We appreciate it even when we don't say it."

The Guzzi brothers truly had been gifted with parents that made all the difference in how their lives, loves, and futures were shaped. Marcus was never more aware of that fact than while he was beginning his own life and forever with Cella, and his parents were there at every step of the way with the same support as always.

The same *love*.

It never changed.

He could hear the smile in Gian's voice when he replied, "I know, Marcus. I'll let you go. Enjoy your first night there. I doubt the place will ever be *that* quiet again. Take advantage. And give Cella my love, of course."

"Of course," he echoed.

It was only after he had ended the call he went in search of Cella within the large, quiet mansion. He was unsurprised to find her getting ready for bed in the room they had decided would be their master bedroom.

The bedroom, attached bathrooms and walk-in closets hadn't been the home's original master suite, but Cella liked how it was positioned. So did he, really.

It faced the front of the house with windows that overlooked the property. It was also set between large bedrooms on the same floor that she said would be perfect for their kids and allow them to be close while they were young and needed them at night.

Cella stood next to the ornate, four-poster bed that they had covered with two blankets he kept in the back of the car just in case. Canadian weather was hell in the winter, and one never knew when they might need something extra to keep warm. He kept supplies—like the blankets— in the trunk regardless of the time of year. It proved useful today.

With her hands flat to her stomach, and her body still while her eyes were closed, Marcus took in the scene with a curious eye.

"You okay?" he asked.

Cella didn't open her eyes.

She *did* smile. "Yeah."

"What are you doing?"

"Feeling."

"Feeling *what*?"

"The babies." She did look at him then, eyes wet with unshed, happy tears. Love stretched his smile wide, matching hers, when she said, "They're moving. It's the first time I've felt it and *known* it was them, you know what I mean? It's a bit earlier than when I first felt Tiff, but there was only one baby then, right?"

No, he didn't know at all.

But he wasn't the pregnant one.

"Come feel," Cella said, waving his way.

Marcus didn't need to be told again. By the time he had his palms flat to Cella's stomach under her loose blouse, her face was back to the previous calm determination while she waited. He waited, too, not minding a bit.

But then he felt it.

Barely.

Not something he could describe *well*. It almost felt like bubbles bursting under the surface of her swell, as faint as it was.

Cella let out a quiet gasp, her gaze snapping up to meet his. "There—*that*. You felt it, right?"

Before he could answer, it happened again.

And again.

The two of them started laughing until Marcus leaned in to take a kiss from Cella while she looked as beautiful and happy as she did right then. He wanted to remember that second forever. How her face lit up with absolute joy as she stood in the room that would be theirs, growing their children and giving them life.

He needed that memory.

Forever.

43.

Cella

"THEODORE?" Jordyn asked. "You could call him Teddy as a nickname. Oh, but then what would we call the other twin ... What's a good *T* name, Lucian? A strong Italian name to match Theodore. Catrina is so much better with names than me."

"*No one*," Lucian interjected, pointing at his wife from where he sat across the private church suite, "is calling my grandchild *Teddy*, Jordyn. Not even you."

Cella had to press her lips together to keep the laugh inside at the way her mother glared at her father.

"Lucian!"

"What? I said what I said."

"It's a *nickname*."

"It's *Teddy*," her father spat back. "Jesus, he's not a teddy bear. Be done with it. No, Theodore is out of the question with that kind of nickname."

"First of all," Cella tried to say, "we don't know the sex of the twins yet, keep that in mind. And you're both only picking *boy* names like we might not need girl names. Still a possibility!"

They paid her no mind.

Mostly.

She was also lying. They *did* know the babies were boys but neither she nor Marcus had announced that news to their families yet. They would ... soon. Her mother was just *very* convinced that the twins would be boys, and she was not giving it up.

Her mother held up a hand, silently asking her to be quiet while she stared down her husband. "Well, if you're the master at picking baby names, what ones would you choose for the twins? Theodore was just *one*, give me another. Cella wants the same starting letter for both babies, so give it some thought. I'll wait."

Lucian spluttered as he attempted to come up with a fast retort. "Well, I—maybe something in the family … it's *Cella's* decision, Jordyn! We're not picking her children's names."

"Thank you, Daddy," Cella said, not bothering to hide her giggles any longer. "That's what I have been telling Ma for the last two months."

The playful glowers her parents tossed back and forth— while the hairstylist finished brushing out the soft, romantic waves she had wanted for her wedding day—had Cella smiling. While they had gone forward with a *large* wedding, because she understood that's what was expected of Marcus being the last and also oldest of his brothers to be married, not to mention his position in his family's business, she also wanted *this*.

Time with her parents. A private room just for her and them. Quiet. Moments alone, away from the rest of their large family and the guests. She didn't want to be bothered by last-minute details or problems when all she asked for with this day was to be married to the man who had her whole heart.

No stress.

No worries.

Just love.

That was it.

That's all she asked for.

And like with everything else, when she asked Marcus to provide something, he did it without complaint or even an issue. He made it look *easy*. She wasn't silly enough to think that everything in their life would be as simple and stress-free as the last three months had been leading up to their wedding. Yet, she had the distinct feeling Marcus would still make every effort to try. He was that kind of man.

Amazing.

She was beyond lucky to say he was also hers. After today ... he would be hers forever. She couldn't wait.

For most of the morning, Tiffany stayed and readied with Cella until one of the girl's aunts came with cousins in tow to keep the girl entertained. Hopefully, they would keep her busy and *clean* until she had to do her walk down the aisle with her flower basket in hand.

Once Cella arrived at the church, it was her mother who helped her into the wedding gown that she had picked last minute because her bump kept growing so fast that it would have been pointless to buy a dress more than a couple of weeks out from the wedding date.

Her dress was perfect, though.

The color of pink cream over top layers of white tulle and silk, the empire-waist sat just high enough to show off her growing midsection while also being classy and appropriate for the day. The capped sleeves and the scalloped neckline that dipped low on her chest fed her desire for details without being overwhelming. Buttons made of pearls started from halfway down the skirt and closed the dress all the way up her back.

She loved it.

Truly.

"Cella?"

The call of her name drew Cella from her thoughts. Across the room, her mother watched her with a soft smile while the hairstylist began to pack up her things. She would need to move into the next room where another three stylists and estheticians were working on Cella's bridesmaids—her sisters.

"Yeah, Ma?"

"There she is," her father murmured.

What had Cella missed?

Her unspoken question must have shown on her face. Jordyn passed Lucian a wink and smile before saying to her daughter, "You were just ... very quiet over there for a second. We got worried."

Oh.

Yeah.

"Don't be," Cella told her mother. "Today is the *best* day. I'm so happy."

"Are you?" her father asked. "You're not sad at all? Not about William, or even—"

"I went to visit him yesterday with Marcus after the rehearsal dinner. We took roses and stayed a while."

She had a sad moment, then. Safe with Marcus. Today was not about that. She would miss her first husband for the rest of her life, and she would never stop grieving the life they could have had together and how his loss affected *everything*. But at the same time, she had found a new love and happiness with Marcus, and she was unwilling to let her sadness undermine the joy in her life.

They could both exist. She was the only person who decided which one could be present at any given time.

"Are you ready?" Lucian asked, smiling.

He didn't ask because it was time for them to go downstairs, she knew. It was rhetorical. The same question her father had been asking for years every time Cella came to another pivotal life moment where she had to step up and make big choices. The kinds of choices that would change everything.

"Yeah, Daddy," she replied, honest and open-hearted, "I am so ready."

• • •

They had chosen a pastel pink and white as their colors. The church had been bathed in the hues with silk runners, bright bushels of flowers, and tulle strung between every pew.

Her father walked her halfway down the aisle, and Cella walked the rest on her own. Lucian hadn't been offended when she asked if he would mind allowing her to walk herself the rest of the way.

After all, choosing a second marriage really had been a decision that was all her own. She wanted to walk to the man waiting at the end with the same purpose and assurance that she was doing it because she absolutely, entirely wanted to. Not just for herself but for him, too.

Marcus met her at the end with a hand extended, waiting for her to join him. The second she did, the church disappeared, and it was just them at the end of the altar with the priest in front of them.

All the people?

Faces she knew.

Those she didn't …

They all faded.

"I love you," Marcus told her as he cupped her cheek in his warm palm; their gazes locked as the priest began the ceremony. *"Ti amo, sempre, mia bella.* Always, Cella."

He didn't need to tell her. Not when he had already shown her time and time again.

But still …

"Forever, Marcus," she promised back.

44.

Three months later …

BETWEEN all his brothers, his father, and the other men in Marcus's life who had wives that experienced pregnancy … he had been warned there might come a time when his wife's interest in him, and sex, could wane. Because that was to be expected. Growing life was an exhausting business. It took a lot from a woman's body.

He understood that.

Yet, Marcus found that wasn't the case at all with Cella. Or maybe it was just … *him*. Because the bigger his wife became, growing their children inside of her, the more difficult he found it was to keep his hands off her.

She was beautiful.

Glowing.

The very definition of life.

If that wasn't enough to have him constantly hard and panting after his wife then nothing would. Although, Cella didn't seem to mind. Being pregnant with twins hadn't stopped his wife from enjoying sex in the least. If anything, it allowed him to become a little more creative at times to make things work.

Cella's favorite was still being fucked while on her side, with Marcus tucked in tight at her back. That way, he could still get his hands between her thighs—or *wherever*—while he loved her. She could hear every one of his whispers and praises. He could still steal her kisses and swallow her sounds.

He made sure she was loved and adored every single morning. At night, too, if she wanted. His wife wanted for nothing—not when he could read her desires before she

206

even had to open her mouth.

Marcus liked to think it was because, for his whole life, he wanted *that*. Love. He wanted to find a woman that he would cherish in the same way his father did for his mother. He spent all those years learning how to treat the most important woman in his life. So, when he finally had his wife at his side and in his bed every single morning, he made sure she never left it without a smile on her face.

And happiness in her heart.

It helped, too, that the doctors encouraged sex. *Good for pregnancy*, the doctors told them. Add that on top of the fact he just wanted to have his hands on his wife as much as possible, and frankly, they probably wouldn't have left their bedroom at all.

But life called.

Reality waited every day.

They had a family to take care of, business to handle … babies to bring into the world.

Marcus wasn't surprised that his children—his twin boys—decided to let their parents know they would make their appearance soon while he was in bed with his wife.

At least, the contractions held off until Cella was sweaty and naked and *loved*. He had to admit, his wife was amazing. For all of it. From the start to the very end. She wasn't scared of the pain. Nothing was too much for her. He had never been more in awe of someone than he was of Cella as she gave him their children.

Leonardo and Lorenzo Guzzi came into the world on a late February afternoon. With twin births, there was always a worry that they would have to default to surgery if something wasn't right …

They were lucky, though.

Everything went exactly right.

Leo came first.

Enzo came second, *crying*. And didn't stop until he was two. Marcus would swear by it.

But he loved them.

Immediately.

At their first breaths.

If his wife was life and love, then his sons became his universe the second they came into the world. Marcus knew right then that while he had been a man before his boys, and he was honored to be a daddy to a little girl that chose him, he became something else when his sons were born.

Their *father*.

It was bigger than being just a man—a boss, made, or anything like that.

It was *more*.

They made him more.

And they came from his wife.

She gave him everything.

Love wasn't a good enough word. But goddammit, it was the only one Marcus had, and it was the only thing he could whisper against his wife's sweaty, tear-streaked cheek in those first few seconds after his sons greeted the world with their loud cries filling the room.

"*Love you, love you* ... *I love you.*"

He would never stop telling her.

Ever.

ABOUT THE AUTHOR

Bethany-Kris is a Canadian author, lover of much, and mother to four sons, three cats, and four dogs. A small town in Eastern Canada where she was born and raised is where she has always called home. With her boys under her feet, a snuggling cat, barking dogs, and a spouse calling over his shoulder, she is nearly always writing something ... when she can find the time.

Find her at www.bethanykris.com

OTHER BOOKS

The After Another Trilogy

One Step After Another
One Breath After Another
One Second After Another

Boykov Bratva

Fractured Ties
Essence of Fear

The Guzzi Legacy

Corrado
Alessio
Chris
Beni
Bene
Marcus
The Firsts

Renzo + Lucia

Privilege
Harbor
Contempt
Forever
Cusp
Renzo + Lucia: The Complete Trilogy

THE FIRSTS

Andino + Haven

Duty
Vow
One Last Time
Andino + Haven: The Complete Duet

John + Siena

Loyalty
Disgrace
John + Siena: The Complete Duet
John + Siena: Extended

Cross + Catherine

Always
Revere
Unruly
The Companion
Naz & Roz

Guzzi Duet

Unraveled, Book One
Entangled, Book Two
Cara & Gian: The Complete Duet

DeLuca Duet

Waste of Worth: Part One
Worth of Waste: Part Two

BETHANY-KRIS

Standalone Titles

Pink
Pretty Lies
Dirty Pool
Effortless
Inflict
Cozen
Captivated
Dishonored

Donati Bloodlines

Thin Lies
Thin Lines
Thin Lives
Behind the Bloodlines
The Complete Trilogy

Filthy Marcellos

Antony
Lucian
Giovanni
Dante
Legacy
A Very Marcello Christmas
The Complete Collection

Seasons of Betrayal

Where the Sun Hides
Where the Snow Falls
Where the Wind Whispers
Seasons: The Complete Seasons of Betrayal Series

THE FIRSTS

Gun Moll Trilogy

Gun Moll
Gangster Moll
Madame Moll

The Chicago War

Deathless & Divided
Reckless & Ruined
Scarless & Sacred
Breathless & Bloodstained
The Complete Series
Maldives & Mistletoe

The Russian Guns

The Arrangement
The Life
The Score
Demyan & Ana
Shattered
The Jersey Vignettes

FANTASY ROMANCE

The Hunted: A 9INE REALMS Novel

Find more on Bethany-Kris's website at
www.bethanykris.com.

www.ingramcontent.com/pod-product-compliance
Lightning Source LLC
Chambersburg PA
CBHW060921180626
46817CB00004B/1342